Bulletproof

Wendy Howitt

First published by Wendy Howitt in 2017
This edition published in 2017 by Wendy Howitt

wendyhowitt.com

Bulletproof

EPUB format: 9781925579741
Print on Demand format: 9781925579758

Cover design by Emmanuelle Harrington

Publishing services provided by Critical Mass
www.critmassconsulting.com

Wendy Howitt is the author of two young adult books, USER PAYS and BULLETPROOF. She has written on staff for Vogue Australia, Harper's Bazaar and the Sydney Morning Herald. As a freelancer, her byline has appeared in many publications, including Cleo, Inside Out magazine and The Australian Magazine. She has also won two beauty journalism awards.

Chapter 1

Twenty-four hours into the spring holidays and while my friends were hanging out at Westfield I was chained to the kitchen sink. Okay, so not literally. But I was feeling very very *oppressed*. Mum had gone out to one of her save the world meetings and I was in an apron sweating over a hot stove. Actually, I was making a salad at the island bench. It was also kinda chilly for September so not so much sweat going on, either. But you get the *idea*. I was making the dinner for my little sister and her kleptomaniac friend, Paris Knight – her real name, not a joke. On the front of my apron was the slogan *A woman's place is in the struggle not the kitchen*. The irony was *not* lost on me. It had been brought back from a women's refugee conference in Cambodia by my mum. A bra and camisole were drying on a cake rack beside me. I'd also unplugged the toaster to make room for my older sister's hair straightener. Winona was getting ready to go out with her boyfriend, who worshipped straight hair.

That left me babysitting Katy and Paris, who was staying over, because we had an early start tomorrow – we were driving to Paradise Caravan Park for our annual holiday. And, get this, my Mum, who refuses to buy into conventional standards of feminine beauty by not shaving, thus allowing small mammals to live in her armpits, nor colouring her steel grey hair, had agreed to take Paris with us on holidays so Mrs Knight could have a *cosmetic* procedure.

Hypocrisy in this family is *rife*, I huffed to myself as I turned my underwear and liberally dressed the lettuce leaves (I liked vinegar). The light of the hair straightener blinked on: ready for action. If mum were here she'd make me go all the way to the bedroom to inform Winona. But since she wasn't I shouted it without moving from the kitchen doorway. Not surprisingly, there was no answer. Well, too bad. Winona's hair could stay frizzy. I pushed my own back grimly and added sultanas – a fibre tip from an old *Australian Women's Weekly* cookbook – to the bowl.

My sisters were going to have to get used to a new way of doing things if Mum is going to leave me in charge for three days at Paradise Beach Caravan Park. I'd never babysat for more than three hours before, but she was confident I could do it. Mum was a big believer in independence and thought it was never too early to learn life skills.

"How can we expect you to become well-adjusted, effective adults, if we don't let you practise these things as children," she always says. Not that she had a choice – the government was hardly going to check the Taylor calendar before scheduling a Save the Universe conference.

"And, in any case, you won't be completely alone. There's the office during the day and you can always go to Sheila at night if there's a problem." Sheila was Paradise Beach's oldest, if not wisest, resident and a great friend of mine. "And I'm only a few hours away in Canberra." And I was getting paid.

It didn't stop me from complaining.

"It's child labour. That's what it is. It's socially unjust and a form of torture which I'm pretty sure is illegal in this country," I said loudly over the morning's toast and orange juice.

"You are not a Bangladeshi child labourer. You are a young woman from a first world country being paid good money to spend time with your sisters at the beach," said Mum in the voice she used on ministers and CEOs.

"I think we should clarify the definition of *good*," I said. I also didn't see why I had to be the one to babysit when I had a perfectly available older sister.

"You know she can't. She's got to study if she wants to do well." *Bloody* HSC.

I tried another tack: "What if I want to go to the beach, hang out with Jess or, like, have a life?" Jess was my best friend from Paradise and she would be the first one to tell me to shut up. I could almost hear her voice in my ear, "Stop complaining. You're on a good thing. I would kill to have your parents, the way they let you just get on with things, make mistakes. Mine have to control everything I do, drives me crazy." She was a girl who had chafed under adult supervision since the age of five.

"Can't you take them with you?"

I shot Mum a look of disbelief. She sighed.

"Do you think your labour is worth more than … what exactly am I paying you?"

"$50 a day."

"You'd like more? Tell me what you think would be fair."

I stared thoughtfully at Katy who, throughout this conversation, had been tugging her lower eyelids down with her forefingers and flapping her tongue around in a disgusting manner.

"A gazillion dollars might do it. Just."

"Very funny. How about $50 a day and $50 each night?" Mum took out her right earring which meant that she was getting ready to talk on the phone and our discussion was nearly over.

I ran the numbers in my head, 250 bucks. That should just about cover it.

"Deal." I would have made her shake pinkies on it but she had already left the room, her phone glued to her ear.

Now, Mum was long gone, dusk had settled and as I listened to Katy hollering, *my daddy … mhuh mhuh whah* … at the top of her lungs, I wondered if I shouldn't have pushed for $100 per day; maybe mention minimum wage and the equal rights commissioner. Except she was a friend of Mum's and probably would be on her side. Katy's voice rose up, *mhuh mhuh whah*. I put my hands over my ears. I couldn't stand Taylor Swift. I preferred my music gutsy and raw. *Real.*

It was going to be a long night.

Slam, crash, pop. What was that? I wrapped a scarf – the stripy one Winona made for me in design tech a few years ago – around my neck and made my way down the hall. I gingerly opened her door and saw my sister leaning out her open window in just her bra and underpants eating from a packet of Cheese Puffs.

"I can't believe you're doing that?"

Winona put another Cheese Puff in her mouth. "What? Hanging out in my room?"

I came all the way into the room. "No, eating crap."

She held out the packet. "Want one?" I shook my head. I had to get into a bikini tomorrow. Winona returned to the business of eating.

"Has Carolyn left yet?" Winona had taken to calling my mother by her first name. I wished she wouldn't. It made it sound as if we didn't have a mother.

"Ages ago," I said watching as she licked cheesy crumbs from each slender finger. "What will Sinclair say?"

"About what?"

I stared at her. Was she serious? Sinclair Reed, Winona's boyfriend was not only *hot*, he was perfect and totally into her. But he didn't approve of her eating junk food. He didn't let it pass his lips either. He said it interfered with his training. Mr Perfect was fanatical about his fitness. When I was in my cross-country running phase, he let me jog with him around the bay. I'd wheeze, just about, all the way around, but he'd barely break a sweat. We'd complete our session with chin-ups, lunges and squats, the whole routine, at the muscle park at the tip of the bay where he'd offer me advice on sit-ups and crunches, and snippets about his relationship with Winona, who he said was the love of his life. He'd lift himself up and down at least 40 times, bam, bam, bam, showing me his biceps – his guns – afterwards. They were, like his shoulders, pretty impressive. He belonged to the intervarsity rowing and rugby teams at Sydney University where he studied science. He wore checked button-down shirts and aviator sunglasses. He looked like Justin Bieber with his shirt on, Chris Hemsworth with it off, and had $10,000 worth of straight teeth that he flashed all over the place. He carried the groceries inside for Mum, taught Katy how to play *Call of Duty* on the Xbox and took care of huntsman spiders in the bath. Like I said, he was perfect. And if there was something about the way his eyes devoured Winona whenever she was in the room, we didn't particularly notice. We were used to it. Boys were always devouring Winona with their eyes.

Winona tipped up the packet to chase the final crumbs. "I'll clean my teeth before he arrives."

She scrunched up the packet and I knew exactly what she was about to do: toss it into the tall canopy of the frangipani tree looming up from the courtyard.

"Don't you dare," I said. I hated litter bugs. I mean, where does all the rubbish end up? The Antarctic, that's where.

"Oh, yeah, I forgot. You're saving the world," said Winona. "Just like Carolyn."

"I'm an environmentalist," I corrected. "And there's nothing wrong with that," and moved swiftly on to my second favourite topic, nutrition. "Did you know that there's not one bit of dairy in those Cheese Puffs?"

Winona pulled the shuddering window down. "What did you say you wanted?" She'd heard it all before. She lobbed the lurid orange packet at her overflowing wicker bin. It missed and unfurled making little popping noises on the floor.

"I want to know if you've got a flirty sundress I could borrow while we're away?"

I caught the pucker of bemusement on her face.

"I know, so *not* me."

I was more of a denim shorts, oversized T-shirts printed with ironic Disney characters kind of girl. "I'm working from this list I found online, you know, essential pieces for resort holidays, yada, yada."

I wandered over to her dresser, submerged my finger in a chipped Limoges cup she used as a vase for droopy peacock feathers. "So I'm on the look out for flirty sundresses and bikinis, cheeky sarongs, that sort of thing." In other words, clothes that appealed to owners of Y chromosomes rather than Japanese exchange students; clothes that Winona wore.

I retrieved a pair of gold hoops from the cup and held them up to my face. "Could these be me?"

"I thought I'd lost those," Winona said, reaching out and almost knocking over a silver-framed picture of her and Dad at her last birthday – her 17th. He gave her a Tiffany bracelet that Winona put on straightaway and never took off. Mum gave her a first edition of the *Beauty Myth* that lay untouched underneath her bed.

Our dad had left six years earlier to live with his personal assistant, now life partner, Gary, in Surry Hills, leaving my two sisters and me with our mother. That she took it badly is an understatement. But she kept going in a cold and brittle way. It was as if he'd never been and it made Winona, who was his favourite, mad. Winona remembered living with Dad best, and missed him the most. Katy had only been six when Dad left and, from the first, called Gary Dad, too, which kinda annoyed Winona.

Gary was okay; he sang, loudly and off-key – like me – in the shower, but cool old stuff like Red Hot Chili Peppers and Oasis; thought that there was nothing a jigsaw puzzle couldn't fix; and taught me how to make béchamel sauce when we were over for one of our regular Friday night dinners.

Sinclair gave Winona BridgeClimb tickets for a sunset tour for her birthday. At the top, I knew from one of our jogging sessions, he planned to give her the world, an achingly romantic gesture that appealed enormously to me. Not that I'd admit it to anyone except, maybe, Winona.

I handed over the earrings, sniffed one of her scented candles and caught the aroma of figs and watermelon and grease. "Want me to light this?"

"Here. Use this." Winona tossed me a sleeve of matches that had the name of a well-known nightclub on it. I went through one, two, three matches before I got it alight.

"About that dress? Can I borrow one?"

"Sure." Winona aimed a vague hand at her wardrobe. She was always generous with her stuff. "Take the floral one. It will suit you."

"Thanks." I put it on, over my cut-off jeans. The scarf dangled out from underneath. I still wore Uggs.

"What do you think? Flirty enough?" I said, twisting my shoulder so I could see Winona's reflection in the glass at the same time.

"If you're a folk singer trying to pick up at a festival, then yes."

I picked up a hairbrush for a microphone and sang the only folksy song I knew, *Kumbaya*.

"Stop that before I throw up my Cheese Puffs."

Obligingly, I put down the brush microphone. "Where are you going with Sinclair?"

"Liam's having a farewell thing-y for me. He and Sinclair have been making jelly shots all afternoon."

"That's nice of Liam since you're only going away for three nights." I had only met Liam once. He wasn't as good looking as Sinclair.

"Why isn't Sinclair having it? The party, I mean."

Winona shrugged. "Sinclair's shitty because I'm going away without him." I knew he wasn't allowed to visit us in Paradise. Winona needed to study if she was to carry on the T tradition and attain the University of Sydney academic medal like Mum did.

"Sounds like fun. I should come. Sinclair wouldn't mind," I said, although, if I was honest, and I tried to be at least once every day, I wasn't so sure. Sinclair was a bit unpredictable that way. I ran my finger across her dresser collecting dust. "Only I've got to babysit."

"Right." Winona was only half listening. She sat, stroking her hair absently, her eyes unfocused, her mind someplace else. Eventually, she pushed off the sill and joined me at the mirror. She dipped her finger in a tub of gloss and ran it around her lips. When she finished, she wiped her finger on a stained tissue, balled it up and threw it back on the dresser along with several other used tissues – Winona was as messy as she was beautiful.

"Paradise Caravan Park. What a joke. With no phone coverage, it'll be hell on wheels more like."

She moved gracefully over to her wardrobe and began to get dressed into a sheer top that showed her bra and a tight pair of spearmint jeans.

"Being unplugged will be liberating," I declared.

I was quite sincere about this. I had recently joined Turned Off, an anti - social media movement. I often quoted from their manifesto such alarming facts as 'screen time before bed drops melatonin levels by 22 percent', to the disgust of Katy. Only this morning,

I announced that I would be taking down my Facebook page. Katy stalked from the room to inform her 349 Instagram followers that her sister was cray cray.

In the candlelit haze of her bedroom, Winona snapped the button on her jeans. "I really don't see why I have to go. I'd be much better off here, at home, studying." She stuck a shoe under my nose. "Boots or wedges?"

"Boots. Why are you telling me? You should be talking to Mum." I sat on her bed and kicked off my Uggs to strap on the wedges she'd just cast aside. Winona had a point about one thing: our rusty old caravan was hardly paradise.

"I would if she were here." Winona sprayed the air in front of her with Daisy, that fruity meadowy fragrance by Marc Jacobs that always made me think of labradors and scratchy tartan picnic rugs, and walked through the mist. A drop or two got into my nose and I sneezed like a cat meme.

"It's called our annual family holiday for a reason. You have to go. Mum said so."

Winona, completely aware of the usual Carolyn irony of this, given the fact that Mum wasn't even staying, cocked one eyebrow meaningfully.

"Yeah, yeah," I said in response. "Anyway, I don't know why you're complaining. You're not the one minding the Terrible Two."

"Right," said Winona. "This will be such a relaxing break for me."

"Okay, so this is not a family holiday then," I said. "Maybe we should call it a working holiday."

"Let's leave out the holiday part altogether," said Winona, attaching the gold hoop earrings I'd recently held up to my own round face.

I eased off her perilous shoes and squished my feet back into Uggs, even though my toes were getting a bit sweaty. She was right. This would be no holiday for either of us.

"I'm a bit scared that we're staying on our own. I didn't go so well in my last first aid test," I said.

"You watch too much *CSI*. If we don't die of boredom, we're going to be fine." Winona closed her dresser drawer with force. "How much trouble can two little girls get into in a hick place like Paradise. There isn't even any wi-fi."

"Uh, if you don't count drowning or burning the place down, then none." I went over to the window, opened up and leaned out to inhale the dusk and an early frangipani flower, the promise of summer. Over the top of a million twittering birds in the nearby bay park, I heard the sound of a car pulling up out front.

"Sinclair's here," I announced and waited for him to get out of the car: like I said, my sister's boyfriend was serious eye candy. But he didn't. He kept the engine running and rested on the horn instead, causing me to wince, and Winona, who was running her fingers through her hair, to murmur, "Cool your frigging jets." She gave her lips another slow coat of clear lip gloss, taking her time with it even though we both knew that Sinclair hated to be kept waiting for anything. Winona was 20 minutes late to everything.

Beep. Beeeep. That horn again.

Winona tapped the side of her head. "The monsters aren't always under the bed."

"Yeah, yeah," I said. But I didn't have a clue what she was talking about.

Winona stepped back to regard herself one final time in the mirror. "How do I look?"

I didn't need to even glance at her to know. With her luminous skin, doe green eyes, caramel hair and even longer golden limbs, Winona was very beautiful, made up or not. I should know. I've had to share a bathroom with her for 16 years.

It always came as a shock to other people. Once when we were on the Westfield escalator a man caused a ruckus clambering over people to hand Mum his business card. He was a model's agent and had spotted Winona in the crowd. He was desperate to have Winona on his books. Mum tore up the card immediately, and said in her iciest drawl, "Over my dead body," as the scraps of paper fell about our feet and those of the open-mouthed onlookers.

"Do you want me to save you some dinner?" I blew out the candle and followed her out of her room, downstairs and into the hall to see her off, and wave to Sinclair.

But it was Liam standing at the front door, squinting through the glass window at the side.

"You're Winona's sister. Er, Katy, right?" *Katy?* I was seriously offended.

"Maddy," I said coolly.

"Sorry. I shoulda known. She said you looked alike. I'm Liam. Winona, is she, like, ready?" He shifted a little on his feet. He was wearing scuffed Vans and one of his laces was undone and frayed. I peered past his shoulder at Sinclair's elbow, resting on the window frame of his father's frosted blue Mercedes, his fingers tap, tap, tapping on the steering wheel. He dipped into view as he checked his orthodontist's work in the rearview mirror and glared at our front door.

"Tell your sister to hurry up," he mouthed. I gave him the thumbs up sign and pivoted to find out what was keeping Winona. But there she was, right behind me, in the hall.

She looked at Liam.

He smiled down at her. "Hey, you," and opened the door wider to let her through under his arm. Halfway through, she stopped and I saw her arm snake back behind her. We touched hands through space, the secret Taylor shake, sliding our fingers all the way down to the end.

"See you, Mads. Don't wait up," and she was gone.

Chapter 2

The house felt empty without Winona. Loneliness washed over me like … like … sea foam. Very poetic, but how silly to feel like that. I shook myself free of it and went in search of Katy.

I found her in the living room with the music cranked up, dancing around Mum's super expensive Italian glass coffee table in Winona's wedges, which she'd swiped from her bedroom floor.

"Join me," waggling her butt. I thought twerking was, like, O.V.E.R.

"No, thanks, I value my self-respect," I said turning down the music.

"Hey. I'm dancing to that." Katy lurched over to the iPhone, tripping on the edge of the Persian rug. She grabbed my shoulders to steady herself. I pushed her gently away.

"Does Winona know you're wearing her shoes?"

"You know she doesn't mind about that stuff." Katy put her hands on her hips, dipped them down,

"How do I look?"

"Ridiculous, obviously, since you are a kid with braces, not a 25-year-old exotic dancer."

I picked her up by the elbows and plonked her down on the couch.

"You'd better have finished packing."

"Who are you? My mother?"

"If I was, I'd have put you up for adoption long ago."

"Very funny." She poked out her tongue, slid off the couch and became distracted by the sight of her reflection in the cathedral window behind the credenza. I sat in the warm spot where she'd been and watched her. My little sister, Lady Gaga stuck inside a Cabbage Patch doll, was a handful, had been so since birth; a girl of extreme emotions, who made me in turn fiercely protective and frustrated as hell.

"What's for dinner?" she asked, sliding a hand inside her uniform to adjust a lacy bra strap – Winona's – holding up the flattest chest you ever saw.

"Thai beef salad," I answered, knowing better than to mention sultanas and fibre, two of Katy's least favourite things.

"Really?" she said. "Yuck."

"What's wrong with that?" I was huffy. My culinary skills had greatly improved since I'd first served frozen chips and Betty Crocker brownies for dinner. Dad had done most of the cooking, mostly out of necessity because when he married her, Mum could barely boil an egg or toss a salad. After he left, Mum bought a slow cooker which she filled in the morning before work, but half the time forgot to turn on. We then switched to microwave meals until Katy gave herself third degree burns on a nuked lamb korma. A series of nannies followed until we were old enough to be left with just Winona. Problem was that she thought chewing gum was a food group.

One day, while waiting for the pizza boy to deliver our dinner – and his phone number for Winona, who would never use it – I found an old *Australian Women's Weekly* cookbook shoved at the back of a cupboard and began to experiment with stroganoff, savoury crepes, salmon mousse and devils on horseback which were immediately spat out by Katy. I progressed to the 21st century and Jamie Oliver and fresh produce, choosing ingredients mostly from the bottom of the food pyramid rather than the top.

"Just for once, can we eat like normal people?" Katy pushed her cleavage together.

"We are." I pointed to her chest. "Since when did you start wearing a bra?"

Katy, focused on pushing tissues into its cups, didn't reply. Finally satisfied, she turned this way and that to admire her new unnatural curves.

"Does this make me look older?"

I let my exasperation hiss through my teeth.

"It makes you look something, but older is maybe not the word."

"Paris and I are getting boyfriends these holidays."

I got the impression they weren't planning to be discerning with their selections.

"You do realise you're only 13."

"Nearly 14." Katy gave me a sideways smirk. "Do you think you'll snare Matt Armstrong this year? Otherwise, I might take a shot."

"Don't you dare." I threw my tea towel at her big, fat head. "Anyway, as if he'd look at you?" Matt Armstrong was the older brother of Jessica, and last year became the catalyst of one hell of a chemical reaction inside me.

"You either." Katy ducked. "Do you think Winona and Sinclair are in love?" Katy pronounced it lurve. "Paris reckons her mother is in desperate love with her gym trainer. She wears Lycra all the time and feels her body morning, noon and night."

"Do you mind? You just made me swallow my own vomit." I didn't want to imagine Paris's mum getting it on with a man half her age. But it would explain the need for a procedure right now.

"Out of my way." Katy swiped up her phone lying on the coffee table. "Gotta keep ma streaks up," and gave another little shimmy.

"Will you stop doing that. It's gross."

"What? This?" Katy shimmied again. "Paris and I downloaded a step-by-step guide on YouTube."

"Does Mum know you've been doing that?"

Katy didn't bother to answer. Our mother, of course, disliked music videos; said they were exploitative to women and a reflection of the media's abhorrent obsession with sex culture.

"Women have brains as well as vaginas," she was fond of saying. I once offered to cross stitch it onto a cushion, which made Winona laugh so hard that orange juice flew out her nostrils. Mum was not amused.

"You should be setting a good example for millennial feminists."

It was my turn to snort. As if that was ever going to help Katy.

"Paris let Harry Mooney get to first base this afternoon even though he smells like old lunch boxes. She's going to tell me all about it tonight." Katy sounded gleeful.

"She is unbelievable," I said.

"I think it's romantic." Katy's eyes gleamed.

"Ridiculous is what it is. And totally inappropriate."

"You're just jealous."

"What? Of having my name and number written in the boys' toilet?"

"That's my best friend you're talking about. And it wasn't even her number. It was the local police station," shimmying at me, "So, ha!"

"Will you stop doing that," I said, shielding my eyes and backing out the door.

Bing went the doorbell. The Kleptomaniac had arrived. Katy and I reached the front door at the same time, Katy, skidding up the hall in Winona's heels and me with a smile nailed to my face in the event Paris's mother, with her hard body and even harder face, wanted to talk to a responsible person. But all I caught was the tail lights of her Cayenne as she roared off. Can't keep a stud muffin waiting.

There was no sign of Mr Knight.

Squealing, the girls threw down Paris's purple suitcase and kicked off their shoes to jump up and down in the hall like they were on a trampoline. I clapped my hands and, in a voice as crisp as cellophane – I was channelling my Year Six teacher – I told them if they wanted to carry on like that they could go and do it in the bedroom.

"Harry Mooney kisses like a fish," I heard Paris declare as they rushed to the stairs.

"Tell me every little detail," and Katy slammed the door.

It was a long, long night.

* * *

But by 8am our bags were stashed in the boot, the groceries piled up under our feet in the bag and we were on the road, Mum and Winona both with travel cups of coffee in the front. I could smell these even though I was in the back, squashed next to Paris, who put her morning breath all over me making the prospect of 600 kilometres down to Paradise Caravan Park even more horrendous.

Mum spent most of it on Bluetooth arguing with a strident disembodied voice about a keynote speaker who seemed to have a drinking problem. I sat there, wedged in the back, my eyes fixed on the horizon to keep the waves of car sickness at bay. The girls talked too loudly and way too much over the top of my head. They went on and on and on about Harry Mooney until I wanted to wring their necks. Instead, I told them to shut up.

"What's with you?" Katy said. "We're on holidays."

"… force. I say take the committee by force. Carolyn, you're not to put up with this …" The disembodied voice ricocheting around the cabin seemed to have moved from the failings of the keynote speaker and on to a committee coup. Mum's silver earrings moved up and down as she nodded.

Winona sat beside her, tired and wan after a late night that ended with a fight at midnight with Sinclair outside our front door that, since I slept in the front room, I half-heard. I had been lying awake in bed, torturing myself with possible scenes between Matt and me. They ranged from I've-just-realised-that-you-

Maddy-are-the-love-of-my-life and I-don't-think-of-you-that-way-we're-just-friends to I'm-in-love-with-someone-else-who-happens-to-be-your-sister. In the middle of a scene in which we run towards each other along the shoreline in slow-motion, I heard Winona's tearful, pleading voice, but I couldn't make out what it was about. Sinclair's voice stayed low and even, but I could tell he was angry. After about 20 minutes, I heard him climb back into his car, slam the door and roar away. I thought about getting up and going to Winona, comforting her or something. I could hear her in the bathroom weeping a little, but then I heard the springs of her bed squeak and her bedside light snap off. I'd talk to her in the morning.

Now, in the car on the freeway heading south, with her head resting on her hand against the tinted glass, I knew there would be no conversation from her. I stared at her profile, perfect even though I could see that she hadn't properly removed her make-up. Dark smudges leaked out like bruises from beneath her sunglasses, splotches marred her neck and her lips were pale and puffy.

"We broke up," was all she said when I leaned forward from the back seat to find out what happened. She didn't open her mouth again the entire trip, not even to answer me when I asked if we could swap seats, even though it was well known that I got car sick in the back.

"Please. I'm feeling sick."

"So am I," Winona said. "I'm getting a migraine."

* * *

It was late in the afternoon by the time we arrived, driving along the undulating road that bisected the park, with its caravan rentals on the right, permanent sites over beyond the amenities block to the left and the patchy ground for tents. These were pitched at right angles like rows of canvas apartment blocks according to the strict bylaws. Rental caravans formed orderly lines just beyond the tents in a grid pattern in which the main path was crossed by rows of smaller paths. Our battered caravan with its striped maroon and green annexe was in the third row. Sheila's caravan was on the other side of the park with all the other permanents.

On the beach, visible from the path, high tide was pounding foamy waves at the sand. Holidaymakers had already dragged folding chairs in front of their caravans, evening drinks in hand, to experience Sunday's sunset and fishermen who hadn't yet given up on catching dinner.

Tired and queasy, we bunched at the door of our caravan, bags knocking into stiff legs and feet already filthy from the sandy path, waiting for Mum to fetch the old-fashioned key from the manager whose head above the reception window always bore an uncanny resemblance to one of Marge's sisters from *The Simpsons* and whose name behind her back was Mrs Hitler on account of her tyranny. Paris, noticing the hairdo, nudged Katy with a snigger. Mum inserted a long finger into the cord lacing of the annexe and finally unlocked the door of the caravan itself. Warm stale vinyl air burst forth making me gag as the door swung open and Mum put it on its latch.

Katy and Paris attempted a swift getaway – "I want to show Paris the games room and where Sheila lives and everything" – and were yanked back by Mum's hands at the scruff of their necks.

"You're not going anywhere, you two, until you've helped," she said, and ordered them to carry in everything from the car. Mum made up the beds, while Winona and I turned on the fridge and loaded it up with milk, bread, eggs, butter, fruit and packets of sausages for frying on the barbecue plate teetering along the side of the caravan.

Mum and I assembled dinner – tinned tomato soup warmed on the tiny stove top, the last of the season's mandarins and packets of salt and vinegar chips – while Winona read Dante's *Inferno* on her bed in the dim green light of the annexe. I thought, not for the first time, that it would have been nice if Winona helped. Not that she'd be any use, really. She was built for show not activity. But I brought it up, anyway, in the dim stark light of the caravan. Mum just said she had to study.

"You might as well start earning your babysitting money now," said Mum as she sorted out the kitchen.

"Do you really think I can do it?" I arranged chips around the edge of the mismatched plates.

"Do what? Arrange those chips? I should think so. It's not rocket science," Mum said, rinsing out the soup tins in a stream of brownish looking water.

"No. Not the chips. Look after Katy and Paris?"

"Honey, of course you can." Mum, looking out of place inside the caravan in her linen shirt and statement jewellery, wiped her hands on a tea towel printed with a cornucopia of marsupials and put her arms around me.

"You're smart, sensible and resourceful. And, you've been babysitting Katy for years."

"But you always came home at the end of the night," I said into her neck, breathing in the clean smell of Bulgari Green Tea, her signature scent, and feeling her hair in my nose.

"You have Winona to back you up. And Sheila's not far away."

"Winona better help me."

Mum let me go, smoothing down her linen shirt.

"I'm sure, when she can, she will."

"Mum? Why didn't you let her model when that guy stopped us in the shopping centre?"

"I want more for Winona than a life that revolves around her looks. She needs a proper education so she can become a valuable member of society and be taken seriously. I want the same for you and for Katy." I rolled my eyes at the thought of anyone taking Katy seriously.

"You are going to babysit them beautifully," Mum said, taking my face between her hands. "You know exactly what to do. And so do they. I have told them to stay within the caravan park at all times unless you are with them. Bedtime is 10pm. They'll have cereal for breakfast, sandwiches for lunch and you've got sausages for dinner which you'll cook on the barbecue. And I'm leaving you plenty of fruit and vegetables."

"I can do this," I said, nodding my wedged head as best I could.

"Yes, you can," Mum said, nodding along with me. "You are very capable. Being an independent and responsible adult is as much about looking after yourself and others as a good education." She pinched me on the cheeks. "Go on, I'll finish dinner."

Feeling better, I wandered into the annexe. Winona was getting ready to take a shower.

"Can I borrow your earbuds?"

"Gross. Why can't you use your own?"

"Yours are better." Sinclair had bought her a super luxe pair from the States.

"Whatever." She threw me her buds and I climbed on my camp bed, the scratchy blanket against my shoulder blades, and scrolled through my playlist until I came to *Grenade*, a classic, and it made me think of Matt Armstrong.

"I wonder who you'll see on the way to the showers," I said, in my most casual manner.

"Nobody, I hope," she said, twisting her hair into a knot and slinging her towel over her shoulder. "I'm *really* not in the mood."

She pushed past Paris and Katy who had returned from their tour of paradise.

"Paris loved Sheila's velour tracksuit, so retro," Katy said. "She says she's going to be keeping an eye on us while Mum's away." She tilted up her nose and snorted. "Like we need supervision." I rolled my eyes.

"I saw that. You're making out Paris and me are out of control."

"Paris and I, dear," Mum said, stepping down into the annexe. "And no one's saying that. In fact, I have complete faith in you and your behaviour in the next few days."

"Thanks, Mum." Katy threw me a triumphant look. "Sheila wants you and Maddy to visit her and tell her exactly what she can do to help. I've already told her not to bother; that we've got this sorted."

I'd visit Sheila tomorrow, I thought, untwisting the cord of Winona's earbuds. Tonight, I planned to torture myself with *Grenade* and think of Matt Armstrong, who I was pretty sure wouldn't even catch a cold for me.

Winona returned, squeaky clean and damp, drying the insides of her ears with a corner of her towel. I sat up.

"Winona?"

"Mmmm."

"Why did you dump Sinclair?" There was no doubt in my mind that Winona was the dumper.

Winona pursed her lips and didn't answer, but there was something I spied on her face, the suggestion of a secret that she hadn't yet shared with me.

"What's going on?"

"What's with all the questions?"

"I don't know. I'm just trying to understand." Why was she being evasive? We usually told each other everything. At least I did.

"I thought you were in love."

"What makes you think I'm not in love?"

She left on that cryptic note to hang her towel on the clothes line that stretched between our camper and the Richardsons.

"How many nappies do you think she has to change?" she said when she returned. She kicked off her flip flops to sink down on her bed. "God. Who'd ever be a mother? Far too much excrement to deal with."

"But you'll marry one day? You know, like Mum and Dad."

"And look how well that turned out." Her voice dripped with sarcasm.

"That's different."

Winona stared at me. "How is it different?"

"Just is."

She waggled her head. "You read too much of that romance shit. Love and marriage is all well and good. But at some point you have to grow up." She began to slap moisturiser on her face and neck and, finally, her hands. "No way am I getting married and having babies at 17. As soon as I can, I'm out of here."

"You sound just like Mum."

Winona glared. "Carolyn and I couldn't be more different."

"Whatever you say." But I was still curious. "Don't you believe it's possible for women nowadays to have it all? You know, career, travel and family. That's what Mum always says."

"Sure. If you're with someone who believes that too." Winona spread out her sarong over the top of her bed, picked up her book and began to read. I tried one more time.

"Is that why you guys broke up? What if Sinclair was willing to catch a grenade for you? Would you get back with him?"

Winona didn't look up. "What are you crapping on about now?"

"This song." I unhooked the earplugs so that the song could be heard in the annexe. "Basically, if that isn't true love, I don't know what is."

"Sounds more like stupidity to me." Winona was short, matter of fact. "If a guy caught a grenade for you he'd die, right?"

"I reckon," I nodded vigorously. Like I said, sooo romantic.

"Well, he wouldn't make a very good groom if he was dead, would he?" Winona ended the conversation by going for a walk and the sound of her slightly mocking laughter echoed for a long time in my ears.

Chapter 3

The next morning, I woke stiff and sore from the narrow camp bed, starving and needing to pee. The drawback of caravan park living was that half its residents were between you and the toilet block. Quietly, so as not to wake the others, I slid out of bed, zippered up my fleece over my pyjama tank, tied up my Converse High Tops and swiped at my nest of hair. I got myself onto the path where I was bombarded with disgusting good cheer.

"Hi."

"Morning."

"It's going to be a corker."

It's 7 in the morning, I thought. Why couldn't people just get on with the ablution business, get it over with, not be so social? Without any Cheerios inside me, I was not at my best as I trod the pathway, head down, hands rammed into pockets, muttering greetings, umm, hi, morning, yeah, great, isn't it, doing my best to get across the park without making eye contact. I barely even registered the games room on my right, with its familiar fart stink, stained vampire novels, leatherette couches grouped around an imaginary fireplace, pock-marked dartboard and ancient Lara Croft pinball machine.

A trail of girls, tweenies, clutching sponge bags with towels wound around their heads like turbans, surged alongside me, aiming for the shower block. Inside, it was packed with half the park, like being in a mosh pit – not that I'd actually ever been in one.

I turned to flee but then spied Sheila at the sink. She was rinsing a teapot and assorted pieces of crockery under the tap.

I loved Sheila. Even though there was 50 years between us and Sheila was a pensioner living in a caravan park and I was a city brat, we got along super well. I sang out her name and hugged her hard. Her open floral overshirt closed over me like a shower curtain and I breathed in her familiar smoky vanilla scent that reminded me of sponge cakes and campfires.

"Hello, love," she said in her gravelly voice, leaning back to inspect me from a distance and then up close.

"Your aura is a little dirty," she pronounced, "but nothing a holiday can't fix." Did I mention Sheila was New Age?

"Thanks, Sheila." I didn't tell her I wasn't sure exactly what an aura was, and jostled my way inside a cubicle. Afterwards, washing my hands, I enquired about her nerves. Last year, her nerves had been one of her favourite topics. We'd spent a lot of time discussing them sitting on her banged-up garden chairs.

"Fine until Stan took up playing the harmonica and shot them to hell." She straightened up. "That man has no musical skill whatsoever."

Who the hell was Stan? Before I could ask, she'd moved on.

"I saw your sister last night. She needs to be careful."

"Don't I know it," I said gloomily. "And I'm stuck babysitting her."

"Dear me." Sheila regarded me with surprise. I stared back.

"Of course, she needs babysitting. You'd have to be crazy stupid to let Katy loose on this place without adequate supervision."

"I wasn't talking about her, dear. It was Winona I meant. She walked straight past me."

My mouth opened a little. What the hell did Winona have to be careful about? She was the lucky one in our family.

Sheila patted my hand. "Come have a cuppa later and tell me about that school play you starred in." Last year, in my *X Factor* phase, I had high hopes of being cast as the lead of *South Pacific* and had practised all my lines on Sheila when Winona got tired of listening to me.

I waved a nonchalant hand. "The acting part was fine. It turns out singing isn't my thing." According to the rest of the cast, I sounded like a choking cat, but there was no point in bothering Sheila with the details. "I've moved on. These days, I'm a poet." Or, maybe a chef, I hadn't quite decided.

"Good for you." Sheila accepted my inconstancy like a true friend.

"The big news is that this time we're on our own. Me, Winona and Katy," I said. "She brought a friend, Paris, you met her last night. Has Mum talked to you yet? She's going to. She wants to make sure that you've got my back which, of course, you have." I held out my hand for a high five.

"A couple of fire-crackers is what you've got there." Sheila, instead of high fiving me, patted my cheek. "You're going to need as much help as you can get."

"Agreed."

"And what's so important that she can't stop here the whole time?" Sheila couldn't fathom my refined and remote mother. She could not comprehend that there was a job more important than raising three girls.

What she failed to understand, and I was only dimly aware in the deepest recesses of my brain, was that she, Sheila, was just the sort of woman that my mother worked so hard to save.

"Something to do with the refugee status of women. She's leaving for Canberra this morning for two nights. It's not far. We can call her if we need her."

"Not much of a reception around here. I've complained about it, of course. But it hasn't made one iota of difference. Not with Madam running the show here." Sheila glared towards the office block. "Thought I might write to the Prime Minister, go straight to the top if you get my meaning. Staying connected is a real problem for us residents."

"Winona thought we'd be able to get a buzz at the northern end of the park." I scrunched the paper towel and threw it in the overflowing bin.

"Maybe. Maybe not," said Sheila, sagely. "Be careful wandering around here. And tell those sisters of yours, too. Crime is through the roof. We've got all sorts of shenanigans going on here. Last week, someone jammed the washing machine slot with that funny looking foreign currency. Out of order it was. For two days. And last night someone stole a sleeping bag off my line." Sheila shook her head. "I've reported it to *her*." She pointed towards the office. "For all the good it'll do. All she cares about is who's cultivating an unauthorised flower garden and who's let their un-transferrable parking space to newcomers for extra cash. But, honestly, the pension is barely enough to live off."

She gathered up her teapot and cutlery, "Don't forget to come across later. I've got something for you."

"Okay." I would give Sheila a rundown of my current writing project. A zine. I might have to explain what a zine was, but I was fairly confident that she'd be interested. She loved a hobby as much as I did.

When she'd gone, I made a space at the slippery stainless steel vanity and peered closely at my complexion through the flickering fluorescent lights in the mirror. Jeesh. Sheila was right, my aura *was* dirty. My hair looked just as frightful. And, was that a blackhead on the side of my nose? I tried to squeeze it between two chipped fingernails, but it hurt too much. What my aura needed was a hit of cleansing ocean spray. Loosening my zipper – the morning sun was getting warm – I picked my way down to the beach, eyes down to avoid the fresh wallaby doo da.

I was almost abreast of the picnic table closest to the main entrance to the beach when I noticed some old guy in a beanie and flannel was already there. I prepared to walk past with, maybe, just an impersonal yet friendly nod in his general direction.

"Hi, Maddy."

I froze, a rabbit caught in the headlights. That was no old guy.

"Er, hi, Matt." I stood there very aware of my frayed hair and dirty aura and the fact that I hadn't bothered with lip gloss or even a brush. Matt Armstrong, of course, when I snuck a peek, looked as gorgeous as I remembered; same sharp angles, monstrously cool hair curling around his neck and drop-dead brown brooding eyes.

"You don't seem pleased to see me," he said, giving me that slow smile that had cursed my dreams, and I was sickeningly reminded of one in which Matt Armstrong became achingly aware that I had grown up into an entrancing woman of the world and was no longer just the annoying friend of his sister, Jess.

"Au contraire, I'm thrilled," I said, brightly so he wouldn't get the impression that I was turning to molten Hg inside.

"You're up early for a non-morning person."

"I am *so* a morning person. A total early bird."

"Huh huh." Matt clearly didn't believe me.

"If you must know, I was just checking out the surf. I might go in later."

I recalled what happened between us last year on the rocks. This same intensity of feeling shot through me now as I gazed at him and, suddenly robbed of air, I collapsed on the bench opposite. It was then I noticed a fishing rod on the table.

"It's a fishing rod," he said, observing the direction of my gaze.

"I can see that," I said, my voice croaky. I cleared my throat and tried again to act normal. "Catch anything?"

He looked me over. "You might say that," and I remembered the state of my hair. Defiantly, I smoothed it down. His mouth twitched, "Stan caught himself a flathead, too."

"Who is this mysterious Stan that everyone keeps talking about?"

"Haven't you seen him? He's the dude in socks and sandals and Hawaiian shirts."

"That's Stan? He owns a budgie that wolf whistles whenever girls walk past, plays the harmonica." He had moved in to the park just before our visit, last September.

Matt grinned. "His budgie contravenes park regulations."

"So does his harmonica playing, apparently," I said. "He once called me a landlubber when I walked past him fishing on the beach." I had the distinct impression it was an insult.

"That's like the worst thing you can be called by Stan. I wonder what you did to annoy *him*?" Matt made it sound like I was annoying to everybody.

"Absolutely nothing," I said huffily.

"Maybe your hair," Matt went on, "He was in the navy, still likes everything shipshape. But what he doesn't know about fish isn't worth knowing."

"How do you know all this?" I said, curious, forgetting that I'd just been monstrously insulted.

The Armstrongs were September regulars like us; the park usually being booked out during January.

"We've been here quite a bit this year."

"Oh, right. So is fishing a hunter or a gatherer type of thing for you?" As a general rule we Taylors were deeply suspicious of anyone who loved the great outdoors. Those rugged types, one minute, were catching lizards or fish, the next, taking the wings off flies and hanging kittens by their necks off clothes lines. I remembered that while Jess and I played by the pool, Matt would go off for hours to fish on the rocks.

"Neither really. I throw 'em back, mostly. I don't know why I like to fish. I think because it lets me think about stuff. It's just you and the ocean. Puts things into perspective, you know?"

I nodded. I knew.

He went on, "It's quiet, no one's talking or being … annoying."

I lifted up my chin. "I think I'll get going then," and made to get up.

Matt put out an arm as if to stop me. "Don't go. I was just kidding."

I sat back down.

"Tell me, are you here with your whole family?" he said. "Is Winona here?"

As soon as he said my sister's name, I felt my eyes narrow to slits and I wanted to slap my forehead for being such an idiot. Of course, that was why he was talking to me. He wasn't finally falling in love with me. Like everyone else, he was infatuated with Winona. I already knew that. Jessica had told me so last holidays when we were reclining on banana lounges by the pool, sucking LOL drinks through straws we'd joined together to make extra long and watching Winona rinse the salt from her hair at the outside showers, the colour of a butterscotch and turning slowly like a ballerina on top of a music box.

I got to my feet, brushed pine needles from my backside. "I'd better go. Say hi to Jess for me. Tell her I'll see her later."

"Oh, right." Matt seemed a little sorry that I was leaving. So what? I squared up my shoulders and with as much dignity as a pair of pyjama bottoms covered in pink butterflies would allow, I stalked off.

Chapter 4

As far as exits go it wasn't a bad one, I thought, as I made my way through the park, passed the closed-up games room and the women's amenities block that was still heaving. My mind was still on the park bench and Matt Armstrong, wondering what had just happened. Sayonara, adios, adieu. That's what.

Okay. I wouldn't have chosen to be in pyjamas, certainly not my pink butterflies. Denim would have made a much better statement; careless and utilitarian; that or slinky black. But, really, it was all the same. I was in control and totally over it. The sun was up, filling the world with glorious, cleansing light. It was a brand new day. If he wanted to lust after Winona, that was his business. He wouldn't get very far, I thought grimly, but good luck to him. One thing was for sure, I would be writing him out of my zine – and my life – as soon as possible. In fact, I'd start right after breakfast …

It wasn't until I was munching my third bowl of Cheerios, pleasantly ruminating over its superior vitamin B content, that I noticed Mum's silver bullet overnight wheelie case standing upright, just inside the door, and it suddenly hit me. Mum was leaving soon and then I'd be in charge. The idea was faintly thrilling in that top-of-the-rollercoaster way. I almost choked on my thiamine, but caught sight of Winona, sitting opposite me, earbuds jammed in. I could tell from her closed expression she wasn't happy and I prayed that Mum didn't want everything to look tidy when she returned. Between them, Winona and Katy could make the house look like it had been turned over by strung-out ice addicts looking for some quick cash.

Mum, already in the mid-blue pantsuit she wore when she was aiming to change people's minds, came out of her bedroom sipping a cup of coffee through reddened lips; her sunglasses perched on top of her head, her oversized red round resin ring, the one we gave her last year, on her pinky finger. Neither she nor Winona were making eye contact and it occurred to me that they had been fighting again. I sighed, pushed back my bowl and leaned heavily into the vinyl seat.

Mum put down her cup to kiss the top of my head. "Honey, don't worry, you're going to be great. Will I make you a cup of coffee before I go?"

"Okay," I said, even though I didn't really like coffee – it brought out my anxieties.

She pushed in the red button of the little white kettle. "I've been to see Sheila. I've also been in to tell the office you'll be on your own for a few days and to ask if you can use their phone if you can't get a signal on your mobile. I know how unreliable it is around here." She passed me the cup, saying, "Careful, it's hot" as I took a sip and grimaced.

"Sugar?" and when I nodded, Mum pushed the bag of sugar across to me, saying, "I've spoken to the girls. They've promised to behave. Yes, I know, it's hard to believe, so ring me if they don't. They've asked if they can go to the beach later – I don't see why not; it's patrolled isn't it? – but they're to tell you when they do."

"Could you tell Katy to give back my bra." Winona spoke loudly to the room in general. Mum frowned.

"Why would Katy have your bra?"

"Katy likes to borrow our bras and wear them stuffed with tissues," I explained.

"What on earth's she doing that for?" said Mum.

I put another spoonful of sugar, and another, in my coffee, "Um, why does Katy do anything?"

"What are we going to do about your bra, Winona?" said Mum. "Are you sure you packed it?"

Winona got up and went to the fridge. She snapped open a tub of yoghurt.

"Course I did. Contrary to popular opinion, I'm not stupid."

Here we go again.

"I never said you were stupid," Mum said. "All I said was that getting into university required hard work and effort."

"Same thing." Winona could be obstinate.

Mum, thankfully, didn't respond. After a minute, she said, "Have you got another bra with you?"

When Winona shook her head, I said, "You can borrow one of mine."

"Thanks, but I don't think it will fit." Winona looked from my ample chest to her regular sized one.

Mum opened her purse, took out several notes and slid them across the table, "For a new bra. And other emergencies."

I gaped, two hundred bucks. That equalled a lot of emergency chocolate.

"Is there a Zara round here?" I squeaked.

Mum ignored me. "Hopefully you won't need this," and more briskly, "Keep it hidden. Not there," as I began to stuff the money into my hoodie pocket.

"Where then?"

"Tuck it inside one of your socks and put it into the bottom of your bag. That's what Sinclair does with anything he wants to keep safe." Winona licked the edge of her spoon.

I did that and returned in time to see Mum drink the dregs of her coffee, put her mug in the sink and drag her sunglasses through her hair to sit them back on the top of her head.

"Better go. My first meeting is at 10 o'clock. Are you going to see me off?"

"You bet." I nudged Winona at the sink. Winona sort of sighed and pushed off to follow me outside. There we stood, shoulder to shoulder, squinting at the sun far off and low in the east, and watched Mum pop the boot and lift in her suitcase. Her silver bangles clacked as she lifted her hand to stroke Winona's cheek,

"Bye, honey. Good luck with the study." I was pleased to see that Winona didn't flinch, though her eyes were lolly hard.

She kissed me before climbing into the car. "Love you."

I nodded vigorously. "Bye," then had a thought and put my hand on the window to slow her down. "Wait. Exactly when will you ring? I forget."

"I'll check in tonight: about six or seven."

"Which?" I didn't want to miss it.

"Hmm, six. Wait, no seven. I might not be finished by six," and she was gone.

Winona went back inside. I sat, alone, on the cold cement block to the side of our caravan my chin in my hand feeling the sun on my cheeks where I'd just been caressed by my mother. I sighed, missing her already. Enough of that. I've got things to do. I dusted my backside and went inside to find Winona.

She was lying on her bed, reading *Wuthering Heights*.

"I'm going to look for the girls on the beach. Want to come?"

"Later, maybe," she said, not looking up.

I left her there to search for my swimmers. While I pulled the floral sundress over my head, I saw Winona's phone lying discarded on the floor. I picked it up and threw it down on the end of her bed, registering at the last second that she'd had six missed calls from Sinclair – I recognised his number – and all made during our drive down. I wondered if I should let her know Sinclair was on the warpath, decided against it on account of her funky mood and threw my towel into a bag which I slung over my shoulder. Part of me wished Sinclair was here right now. He'd have told me to relax and taken me on a beach run where we'd bench press a quick fifty and make Winona cut up a fruit salad with linseeds for breakfast even though she was hopeless with knives and chopping boards and all the food groups.

"Okay, then. I'm going. Bye, now. Have fun with that sexy Heathcliff," – I was a Bronte fan – and left her.

The sun was a sharp prickle on my shoulders as I picked my way over the planks laid out through the scrubby path like a bleached ribcage. I held my breath against the aroma of rotting seaweed and waited for the first glimpse of sea. It coincided with roaring whipping wind that rinsed my nostrils with briny air. I held my hair back with one hand, shielding my eyes with the other. The ocean was clotted with surfers, the beach otherwise nearly empty thanks to the wind, which pressed my dress to my body.

I could just make out two figures in the haze, performing cartwheels near the shoreline. I hiked up my bag and made for them.

By the time I arrived, Katy and Paris had been joined from the other direction by a lanky girl with dark wiry hair, dressed in ripped denim shorts and a black T-shirt, a pair of Havaianas dangling from her fingers. I looked more closely and realised with a jolt that it was Jess Armstrong. But not the Jess I'd left behind last year. This woman with her watchful eyes and sharp shoulders was someone else entirely.

"Hi," I said, suddenly shy which was freaky seeing as we'd always been such good friends and always able to pick up where we left off. I tried a smile. It felt forced, and, anyway, she didn't smile back.

"Hi." She must have felt it, too, because she pushed her hands deep in her pockets and said nothing more. Now what? This was so awkward. I kicked sand around and tried to think of something to say.

Katy, looking on curiously with Paris, said, "You two look like weirdos staring at each other like that."

"Then why don't you run along and play," I said.

"We will. Come on, Paris," and they ran into the wind, screaming like seagulls.

A gust of wind lifted the tangle of hair from Jess's charcoal eyes and I noticed three studs in her left ear and one in her nose. I gave a gasp before I could stop myself.

Jess smirked. "You should see your face. Just like my mum's when I came home from getting it done."

I felt I'd failed the test. "They look ... great," trying to claw back some credibility.

"Check this out." Jess tugged at her top to expose a pierced belly button.

"Looks super cool." I told the lie carefully to hide the fact that my mind was dwelling on the issue of hygiene.

"You think?" Jess sounded pleased.

"Huhuh," nodding hard. "What did your school say?" She and Matt attended an alternative school in Melbourne full of the offspring of actors and artists. "Did they flip out?"

"Nah, they saw it as a form of self-expression, blah, blah." A look of disgust and disappointment flitted across her face. "Not exactly the response I was after."

"You mean ..." I stopped, not sure if I'd quite grasped her meaning.

"Yeah, yeah I was trying to get expelled, or, at least, suspended from poxy school. Next time …" Her voice trailed away, and I could only imagine what she had in mind. Anything was possible with Jess. I took a closer look at her belly.

"Did it hurt?"

"Like hell. But in a good way." Jess looked at me pointedly. "You'd a seen if you were following me on Instagram."

"Ah, yeah, well." I opened my mouth to explain how life passed you by if you were always looking down at a screen, but thought better of that, too. I didn't have to worry. The ice had been broken and we were friends again.

"You missed the best time last night. Everybody hung out in the games room. I saw Winona there for a sec."

"Really?" I sloshed through the chilly water. My thighs felt itchy where drops of salt and grains of sand had collected. I paused to scratch at them. Jessica's voice followed me on the wind.

"Yep. Ben Forbes is totally as hot as ever. You remember him, right?"

I gave her the how-could-I-forget look. I mean, Ben Forbes, a part-time model, would give Sinclair a run for his money in the hotness stakes. Last summer, around the time that I started mooning over Matt, Jess had become totally obsessed with Ben, making us follow him round the park until we caught him kissing another girl in a Tigerlily bikini.

"Ben and Serena have broken up," she said now.

"Really? That's good." I made a sign that I wanted to check on Katy and Paris at the rock pool. Together we sloshed through the frilly water's edge.

"I'm going to make my move this week," she said over the bang of the waves.

Up ahead, Katy pointed to pieces of bubble seaweed over her ears.

"Earrings," she shouted. I put four fingers up across my body rapper-style, the Taylor signal of approval and looked around for somewhere to sit, choosing the place that wet sand meets dry.

"You saw Matt this morning." It was a statement not a question. Jess squatted down beside me. "Did he tell you?"

"Tell me what?"

"About Dad?" she said.

"No." I spoke slowly. "What about your dad?"

"He died."

I stared, appalled, "God. When? I mean, I'm sorry."

"Last December. So, you know, Merry Christmas to us." Jess picked up some sand and let it run through her fingers. I remembered her dad, a handsome man who wore baggy chinos and loose polo shirts and was always on the phone. I couldn't imagine what it might have been like for them staring at all the presents under the tree and only wishing for one thing; their dad back.

"That's awful."

"Tell me about it."

"So what happened? I mean, how did your dad, you know, pass away?"

"Heart attack." Jess was matter of fact as if she was talking about somebody else's father, but I figured that was just her defence mechanism. She'd be pretty messed up. I reached for her hand. She looked at it for a second before she took it. When I squeezed her hand, it felt limp like a squid arm.

"Are you okay?"

"I'm fine. I mean, it's been like hoorrrrendous".

"God, I'm so sorry. What about Matt?" I felt myself flush with shame when I thought about this morning and how I'd huffed off, not imagining for one minute that he might be suffering from grief.

"He had to carry the coffin with our uncles and Dad's business partner, and nearly dropped it." She gave a brief laugh. "It was pretty funny, actually."

Matt nearly dropping his father's body didn't seem very funny to me, but then I wasn't the one grief-stricken. Gulls circled overhead, bickering over a piece of knobbly seaweed. Katy and Paris had come across a tangle of plastic carnations washed up on the beach that had once probably decorated the dining tables of a passing cruise ship and began to make a sea garden, sticking carnations, one by one, in the sand. Paris poked one behind her ear and started capering about.

Jess, looking at them, said, "It's hard to believe we were once that age. I feel so old. I mean, like 100 or something." She let sand dribble through her fingers for a while.

"Do you remember that time we stole a packet of cigarettes from Sheila and smoked them in the sand dunes up there?" Jess pointed at the sandy mounds sprinkled with spiky looking grass. "It gave us headspins."

I groaned, remembering how sick it made us. "I'm never smoking again in my life. Sheila smokes pipes now, anyway."

Really?" said Jess, "We should try it."

I just pulled a face. Jess went on reminiscing. "We borrowed Winona's lipstick, too. We wanted to leave lipstick stains on the butts because we thought it would make us look older." Her laugh was self-mocking. "Pathetic, weren't we."

"And your brother found the packet and told on us to your mum and dad and they hit the roof and wouldn't let us play together for a whole day."

"I was so mad at Matt for doing that." She used a stick to write her name in the sand. She wrote Ben's and giggled.

"And we didn't know what to do with Winona's lipstick so we buried it in the sand back there. It's probably still there."

"I kept expecting her to, like, explode that we had taken it," Jess said.

"Nah, not her style. And, anyway, she didn't even notice."

"How is Winona these days?" Jess kept writing in the sand, random words that collapsed in on themselves. "You know my brother is still obsessed by her."

I noticed that the wind had dropped and suddenly it was hot.

"Oh, really?" I kept my tone light, like I didn't care. A wave unleashed itself onto the shore and the wind drew sharp points across the horizon.

Jess said: "Do you still do all those Buzzfeed personality quizzes?"

"Sometimes. What about you?"

"Nah, they're stupid." She scrambled up. "I'm hot," and began to strip off down to her swimmers – a contrasting bikini – leaving a messy pile on the sand.

"Let's swim. Race you in."

"But it's cold. And there are rips." I called after her. And the beach wasn't patrolled. But she didn't hear me – or ignored me, I didn't know which. I hesitated then took off my clothes, folding my dress and placing my thongs on top. I thought about doing the same for Jess, but decided against it. I was already in danger of being too lame for her as it was. I loosened the elastic caught up in my rump with a sandy – ewww – finger and tiptoed down to the water, letting it dribble between my toes.

"Come in, it's freaking gorgeous," called out Jess. She turned over to float. I sucked in my stomach and inched in. Something splashed my back and I squealed and spun around to be faced by a dog in the shape of a bullet hurtling towards me.

"Oh, my god," I stuttered before staggering out of the way back onto the beach, the sand sloppy beneath my feet. The dog splashed through the water to retrieve a floating stick with its jaws. He dropped it at my feet and shook himself with satisfaction showering me in stinging wet sand.

"Ouch." I ducked away. When he'd stopped long enough for me to take a good look at him, I saw that he was a blue heeler kelpie corgi cross with sawn-off legs and a grey nuggety body. Right now his eyes were fixed on mine, jaws open and smiling, ears at right angles from his head, tail wagging, waiting for me to throw the stick in to the water again.

"Hello, little guy," I said. "Where did you come from?"

It swiped its tongue across my leg as an answer and I stooped to give its grey freckled head a pat. The dog flung itself on the sand beside me, and began to wriggle around, legs kicking, sand flying. I made a visor with my hand so that I could look up and down the beach. I saw a scruffy figure approaching. As he drew closer, I saw that he was about 19 with reddish hair and a three-day growth. There was a yellowish stain that I suspected was egg on his hoodie.

"Sorry about that." He pushed at the dog with a bare toe to make him stop and look at him, upside down, tongue lolling. The dog clambered to its feet and prepared to give itself another almighty shake. I stepped back, really quick this time. The man hauled the dog away by its collar, studded and red. "Stop that. Bad dog," he said, and then to me, "You're covered in sand. You'll have to go in, wash it off."

"It's okay." Something about him appearing out of nowhere made me nervous. I tried to work out where he'd come from. It was a bushy part of the beach about 100 metres from the main park entrance, nothing back there, really, from memory, except for a car park. I brushed at the sticky yellow grains of sand, glanced quickly at him, caught him checking me out.

"Cold, is it?"

As soon as I caught his meaning, I quickly crossed my arms across my chest to cover myself up.

Undeterred, he said, "Here, let me brush it off for you," and moved into my personal space. I stepped back quickly, with a withering stare, but not before I registered his coffee breath – seriously bad. Unoffended, he just stood there still grinning. Whoa, I thought, this guy is creepy and took another step away, towards the sea, and landed on the dog which got him excited all over again. I used the distraction to begin putting on my dress, which caught on my salty skin.

"You staying around here?"

I didn't glance over but sensed he was watching me. I said nothing. He went on smoothly as if he hadn't noticed, "So am I. Perhaps I'll see you around," and he whistled for his dog and headed along the beach towards the point, kicking up sand with his thongs as he went.

"Hey." Jess had come out of the water. She stood, dripping, staring at the guy's departing back. "Who was that?"

"Who knows?" I wrapped my arms around my chest and stared after him, walking away. "Just some wacko," and shivered.

Jess held up her dripping face to the cloudless sky, arms outstretched.

"What do we want to do now?"

"Dunno." I pulled at my dress in the parts that were sticking. I shuddered and thought about the guy with the red hair and hungry eyes, who needed to shave and probably take a shower, too. I shaded my eyes to watch him. He had passed the girls, who were doing handstands, and was almost round the point; I heard him whistle again to the dog, who had paused to bark his head off at the girls' waggling feet. At the sound, he took off up the beach, his stubby body and sawn-off legs pumping two at a time.

"I'd better get these two back, feed them." I used extravagant arm gestures to catch Katy's eye, but she had switched to performing cartwheels, oblivious, so I dug two fingers into my mouth and whistled; one of only two things I'd learned at Cub Scouts.

Chapter 5

We left Jess at the little shop, digging into her pockets for the money for a Coke.

"Want to do something later?" she said. "We could meet at the picnic table near the entrance to the beach. You know the one?"

"Sure."

"Can't we have a Coke, too?" bleated Katy as we crossed the path, in a straggling line, and veered left past the grassy area allocated to tents. There were about six tents dotted about, big family affairs with several rooms but also a few pop-ups for couples. This was not as many as usual, but the first week of the school holidays was often slow.

When we reached our place, I halted. The girls pushed at my back, their warm sandy bodies wriggling like puppies.

"Hurry up, me and Paris want to try out a new dance." Katy kept pushing.

I held her back. "Dust off your feet first."

"Did you check out her piercings?" Paris hopped around on one foot shaking the other.

"What about the one in her nose?" Katy said impressed.

"If it were me, I'd put a really big diamond in there." Back on two feet, Paris pushed her glasses further up her nose.

"I think your mum might have something to say about that." I lifted the flap when I was satisfied their feet were clean.

"She wouldn't care," Paris insisted. "She loves bling."

That'd be right, I thought, stepping inside. Mrs Knight would probably get a good deal on a mother/daughter matching pair of diamonds.

Once inside, Katy took Paris by the arm and led her to the far corner of the annexe where they painted their fingernails snot yellow and discussed in whispers the pros and cons of wearing Spandex in the afternoons. I put the caravan door on its latch and stepped up into the bright kitchen, expecting to see Winona. It was empty.

I poured myself some stale water from the Tupperware jug from the door of the fridge and flopped down on the bench seat. After a while, I became aware of a throbbing pain in the space between my toes where my thongs had rubbed so I kicked them off and went looking for a Band-Aid. Both drawers under the draining rack jammed half way open and I rattled them viciously to make them shut which, in turn, rattled the cups drying. Back in my seat, I applied two Band-Aids, tossing the wrapping onto the table where they slowly unfurled next to a half eaten tub of yoghurt and Winona's discarded copy of *Wuthering Heights*, lying face down on the table, the spine all creased. I picked it up to see where Winona was up to. Heathcliff was covering Cathy with 'frantic caresses' and asking her why she'd despised him.

The story quickly absorbed me and I fell back into the vinyl seat, blisters forgotten, the girls' lunch abandoned, to read.

Over an hour later, the sounds of giggling coming from the annexe roused me like a pinch. I looked up vaguely, my eyes contracting as I exchanged the Yorkshire moors for the beige interior of a mid-century caravan; the bowl of fruit and the frilly curtains at the windows that always reminded me of my old Barbie camper. I stretched. What was the time? The knot in my stomach told me it was late. I threw down the book and began to assemble lunch, pushing aside the strawberry yoghurt to make room for the tiny bread board and a loaf of bread.

The caravan bounced a little with my weight as I worked. I bit into the plastic wrapping of a packet of sliced cheese for sandwiches which I cut into triangles for Katy because that was the way she liked them, and squares for Paris because she always had to be different. While my hands and teeth were busy, my mind was free to wonder about Winona and where she'd got to. Did she want me to make her a sandwich? I couldn't decide. I called the girls to the table and nearly had a heart attack when they arrived dressed to the nines.

I poured two glasses of water and pushed the plates towards them, saying, "You do know it's just a sandwich, not a five-star restaurant?"

Katy took a bite. "This isn't even a one-star sandwich," and after drinking from her cup, "What's with the water, it tastes like fridge."

"Stop complaining or make it yourself," was all I had to say. I didn't even comment when Paris left her crusts. I wasn't her mother: let her have straight hair. When they'd finished, I made them clean up. Afterwards, I passed them each an apple. "Here, eat these somewhere else."

"Like where? Why can't we stay here with you?"

"Don't you have something better to do than to annoy me?"

"Well, there is a volleyball game going … we might do that, I guess," Paris said.

"Dressed like that?"

Paris looked down at herself. "What's wrong with what I'm wearing?"

Er, underwear on show, too much eye shadow, the shortest shorts I'd ever seen … But I settled for a raised eyebrow.

"Wanna come?" said Katy.

"Not really," but I found myself heading around the side of the park to the front of the office where a bunch of little kids were milling around a volleyball court. I nodded to the Richardsons, the Gordons and the Tugwells, all families that had been coming to Paradise Caravan Park for as long as we have.

"Hey, Jarod." I spoke to the nearest Morrison, hoping I got the right one. The Morrisons were a family of four siblings, two boys and two girls although you couldn't tell the difference, ranging in age from 8 to 12, all with long flaming strawberry blonde hair and a reputation for doing anything, I mean anything, for a dare.

"You girls gonna play?" he said. "Sweet." Then, "Let's get going. Where's the ball?"

The ball was up one end of the court with the three Tugwell boys. One of them, the youngest, a skinny kid with white eyebrows, had the ball and was not letting go of it, despite his brothers' hands grabbing for it.

"Just hand it over."

"No."

"Don't be a douche bag."

"Piss off."

"Give us it."

"Not until you say please."

Jarod sauntered up. He was experienced with sibling matters.

"Charlie, let go of the ball. We want to play with it."

"Not until Max apologises for calling me a dickwad," said Charlie, yanking the ball closer to his stomach.

"Max, say sorry." Jarod turned with great patience to Max.

"But he *is* a dickwad."

"He probably is, like my own brother." Jarod was the voice of reason. "But we still need the ball to play the game."

"Piss off, Jarod, and mind your own business." Charlie took himself and the ball further away.

"Dickwad," said Jarod. "Just hand over the bloody ball."

"No."

"Arrrggg." Max, his brother Tom and all the Morrisons fell on Charlie, pummelling and pushing, slapping and giving Chinese burns so that Charlie began to cry, big fat streaky tears. The two dark-skinned boys didn't join in, but didn't try to stop them either. It was like we'd been dropped onto the set of *The Hunger Games*.

"C'mon," I said to Katy and Paris. "Let's get out of here."

"No, I think we'll stay," Katy said, sitting cross-legged on the ground. "See how it turns out."

"Yeah, this is way better than YouTube," agreed Paris.

"Please yourselves. I've got way better places to be. Just be back by 5."

And I left the competitors fighting to the death for some dumb ball.

Chapter 6

Contrary to what I told the girls, I didn't actually have anywhere better to be and I stopped when I got to the fork in the path. One way led to the beach; the other direction, our caravan. I could go looking for Jess or Winona. Or I could visit Sheila. The amenities block out of the corner of my eye reminded me I hadn't showered or cleaned my teeth. A quick sniff of my underarms confirmed this.

Now, a shower in the middle of the day might seem random to most people. In fact, in a caravan park it's a highly strategic move. First thing in the morning, way too busy. In the evening, it's filled with the Teletubbies crowd, even worse. In the middle of the day, when the under four footers are napping and the rest of Paradise is at the beach having a fish or a surf, the shower block is quiet and peaceful. I grabbed my towel and shower shoes – no cooties for me – from the caravan and had the best shower I'd had in days. It was utter bliss.

A skateboard caught my eye as, squeaky clean with a damp towel over one shoulder and my damp hair in pigtails, I rounded the other side of the amenities block. It was leaning up against the brick wall, the wheels all dusty and cracked from overuse on the park's sandy paths. I knew instinctively I was looking at the property of Ben Forbes. Yep, there he was, resting his elbows on the counter, yakking to the part-time guy serving. If only Jess was here. I studied him carefully so I'd be able to report back to Jess in all the glorious detail I knew she'd demand. He finished up and I quickly turned to examine the blackboard specials. Three dim sums for $1. But he must have noticed me looking, the way he ran a self-satisfied hand through spikey hair and sauntered outside into the blinking sun, a Slushie in his hand.

"Hey, Maddy Taylor," he said between bites. When I didn't answer, he flicked me a glance with those blue eyes that Jess was always going on about. A group of his friends loomed up from the path to our left, pulling up about 10 metres away and letting their boards roll between their feet as they waited for him. He raised up his hand in a salute, a casual acknowledgement of his superior girl magnet skills. He then handed me the nearly empty cardboard cone so he could roll off into the distance, "See ya later, Maddy Taylor ..." Making it sound like a promise.

He probably thought I was into him. I dumped the paper cone into the nearest bin. What a nerve. I knew that Jess would be keen for a swift BF update, but something inside me wanted to put it off and so I visited Sheila.

Sheila's patch of real estate was as eclectic as she was, a tangled jungle festooned with tyres shaped into exotic fauna, a rock collection painted in rainbow colours, wooden chimes that banged together incessantly and mollusc shells for ashtrays. The effect was all very haphazard, though Sheila maintained that feng shui principles were strictly adhered to.

As I approached, I heard murmurings coming from the thicket. It sounded like Sheila in conversation. She must have visitors.

I approached cautiously. "Sheila?"

"Maddy?"

"Sheila?" I looked left. I looked right. "Hey, where are you?"

"Here I am." She appeared from behind a palm tree, looking like a giant hibiscus flower on legs and carrying a watering can.

"What are you wearing?" I was used to velour ensembles and pedal pushers but nothing as eye catching as this enormous kaftan.

"This?" Sheila made a ta da gesture, the grand entrance of a star, and turned slowly, the watering can dribbling over her flip flops. "What do you think? I feel like I could be on a cruise ship."

"Fantabulous." I tripped over one of her tyre swans as I attempted to get closer. "Who are you talking to?" I peered into the recesses of her cluttered garden square.

"My ferns, dear." She set down the watering can. "They adore it. Grow like weeds, they do. Last June, I won the Bullawalla garden of the month. There was a photo of it in the local paper. They called me the 'Pensioner in Paradise'. I'm like Eve in the Garden of Eden. Here, let me get you a cup of tea."

While Sheila bustled inside, I sat down on one of her rusty old folding chairs.

Sheila's head popped out of the caravan. "I wanted to plant a cannabis crop, you know, for medicinal purposes," she said. "But old Hitler in the office refused to co-operate."

She disappeared again, reappearing a few seconds later with a battered wooden tray, setting it before me with as much dignity as a person holding a teapot topped by woollen cosy in the shape of a strawberry can muster. I knew it was one of her creations. Sheila knitted all sorts of things to sell at car boot sales in town to supplement her pension. She sat down on the other side. "Threatened to throw me out if I did. Apparently, drug lords don't reflect the park's family values. So I've been on the look-out for a secondary income source."

"Probably for the best," I said. I eyed the brownies on the tray.

"Go on, have one." Sheila pushed the plate towards me.

"Thanks." I took a bite. "These are awesome. What's in them?"

Sheila looked pleased. "I used a secret ingredient. Guess what it is?"

I stopped chewing. "God, it's not cannabis, is it?" and started to spit out my mouthful into a hand.

Sheila gave me a scathing look. "What do you take me for?"

"You were the one who brought up drug cultivation," I said. I eyed the brown goo in my palm. "So, it's okay to eat this? I'm only going to get a sugar hit, not, like, stoned?"

"The only danger is chocolate overdose." Sheila chortled at her own joke. She cut off a piece of paper towel for me. "I made them especially for you girls. Take them back with you. Winona will need one with all that studying."

"If I can find her." I licked leftover crumbs from the palm of my hand. "These are really good, Sheila. Can I have another?"

"Sure, pet," passing the Tupperware container across. "How are you managing with the other two?"

"Okay." I licked around the edges of my mouth. "I guess. They're a bit of a pain. I'm getting paid, at least. Although not enough considering what I have to put up with."

Sheila broke off a piece of brownie, tucked it into the side of her mouth where her dentures were firmer.

"I've got plans for a little something on the side myself," or at least that's what it sounded like; she was a little slurry on account of the mouthful of brownie.

"Like what?"

"I'm getting into the clairvoyancy game."

"What's that?"

"Fortune telling. I'm going to charge $25 an hour to tell people that they're going to fall in love, travel over the seas, get promoted over a nasty co-worker. It will supplement my pension real well. Might even turn into a real career. Get myself some business cards with Sheila the Clairvoyant embossed on the front in fancy gold writing. Don't look at me like that. Some of us don't get cushy babysitting jobs. You should try living off the pension. The pension is peanuts. And if I can't be a drug lord, then I'll be a fortune teller."

"Will you look into crystal balls and tea leaves?"

Sheila scoffed: "Old school."

"Sorry." I didn't know much about the dark arts, except what I'd read in Harry Potter.

"I read tarot cards. And, if you don't mind me saying, I'm a natural."

"They're, like, playing cards but with creepy pictures on them, aren't they?"

"If you mean stunning pictures of queens and cups and swords on them, then, yes. You shouldn't scoff. Who knows? I might tell you that you're going to canoodle with that nice lad from number 148."

"Can you see that in my cards?"

Sheila cackled. "You told me last summer."

"Matt doesn't even like me. He's into someone else." I swallowed and hiccupped, "I'm pretty sure he likes Winona."

"How do you know that?" Sheila said gently.

"Jess told me. Anyway, everyone prefers Winona."

"I don't." Sheila patted my hand with her rough callused one. "I just think you lack confidence in yourself." She gave my hand another pat. "Can I give you some advice?"

"Sure," I said, although I wasn't sure if I was ready to hear the philosophical views of a person who talked to foliage and considered drug lording as a career option. I narrowed my eyes, suddenly suspicious.

"Are you going to charge me $25 for it?"

"I'll give my expertise to you for free. Mates' rates." She smoothed her kaftan over her large knees. "When you make assumptions about what someone else is thinking or feeling, you're usually wrong."

"What else can I do? It's not like I can come out and say to Matt: who do you like better? Me or my sister?"

Sheila nodded. Even she could see the wisdom of that.

"Do you want to know something else?" I went on glumly, "The worst part about it is that I still like him even though I've tried not to and he's probably never going to feel the same way about me. How screwy is that?"

"That's also the most exciting part," said Sheila with a wink. "Especially when it turns out that he does."

I looked at her doubtfully.

"Maybe the best thing to do is to wait and see." Sheila reached for the pot. "Another cup?"

"Yes, please." I downed a second, a third, decided that tea was way better than coffee.

"You said before, you had something for me."

"I'm going to lend you my favourite book. If that doesn't nab you your young man, nothing will."

She returned clutching a dog-eared copy of *Fifty Shades of Grey* to her ample chest and I nearly died of embarrassment.

"Don't look at me like that. A woman has needs." She started to hand it over, then stopped. "If you've already read it, just say so. Raylene from across the path is dying to read it. No? Well, here you go then. Be careful of it, it's my only copy, and I want it back, mind. Stan and I are up to page 154."

"Sheila," I moaned. "That's too much information."

"Don't worry, we're having a break from it. Stan isn't feeling too well right now."

"What's up with Stan?" hoping I wasn't going hear about his prostate or, worse, his Viagra.

"It's Georgie Boy."

I held up two hands. "Stop right there." No way I wanted to hear about Stan's Boy George or whatever the hell he calls his penis.

"Why? Don't you want to know what happened to his pet budgie?"

"What? Is Boy George a bird?"

"*Was* a bird. Not anymore. Georgie Boy is dead. We buried him in the ground over there." Sheila waved to a grassy area behind her.

"This morning when Stan went to feed Georgie Boy his morning chia seeds, he found nothing but feathers on the bottom of the cage."

"Stan just standing there, saddest thing I ever saw. Lost his best friend, he had, and he didn't say a word. Just scraped up the poor little feathers into a cereal box. He's ex-Navy, you know, trained to be poker faced, stiff upper lip and all that. It broke my heart, it did."

She blew her nose. "That someone could do that to an innocent and helpless bird, one of god's creatures. Stan didn't have a clue how it had happened, poor bugger. He loved that bird like he was family. And that's what I told *her*, over at the office, when she tried to have Georgie Boy removed from the park."

"Why did she do that?"

"Because she's heartless, that's why." Sheila clucked her tongue, "Georgie Boy contravened park regulations. And she's a stickler for rules, that one."

"Do you think it was Mrs Hitler exacting revenge." I spoke in a low voice as if Mrs Hitler could hear me all the way from the office.

"She wouldn't get her hands dirty, not her." Sheila puffed up in her chair. "No, it wasn't her. Stan reckons it might have been a fox, they're that cunning, but I have other ideas." Sheila's eyes gleamed. "The other day, I saw a hooligan hanging around. I didn't get a good look at him cause he was wearing one of those hooded jumpers, but he was up to no good, he was."

I felt my skin contract like I'd walked from the sun into someone's shadow. Only this morning I had met a scruffy guy in a hoodie. Unaware of the coldness that had begun to spread though me, Sheila went on, "I reckon he was the one who stole the sleeping bag from my line, too."

Sheila stopped, her watery blue eyes fixed on mine. "Yeah, there are some real sickos out there. And all Madam could do," she jerked her head towards the office, "was say, 'good riddance. The bird was in breach of park rules'. Do you believe it? I'll give her park rules, right up her cabootie."

Sheila's second chin quivered in indignation. "Incredible how a little bit of power can go to a person's head." Emotion got the better of Sheila and she sipped tea noisily through gaps between her teeth until she had calmed down.

"If it wasn't for your boyfriend" – I didn't bother to correct her – "who helped bury what was left of Georgie Boy and taking Stan off for a fish afterwards, I don't know what he would have done."

"The funny thing is, I saw it in the cards when I was practising on Stan. I turned over the devil which means catastrophe."

At least she didn't see the guy with ice cold eyes and a Bacon & Egg McMuffin stain on his hoodie.

Sheila ran on, "I didn't say anything at the time. Wish I had now, might have prevented it."

It was my turn to comfort Sheila. I did so with a pat and a platitude: "You mustn't blame yourself."

Sheila smiled wanly. "I don't really. I'm just a conduit, a conductor of the visions. Actually, I really think I have a gift. After all this time, I can actually do this. At my age, most women are going through menopause, the change of life. Well, I've had a change of life. But at least mine doesn't involve sweats or dry vaginas."

I put my hands over my ears. "That's disgusting. Can we please talk about something else?"

"How about I read your cards," and she hustled inside, returning with oversized tarot cards, several strands of colourful glass beads about her neck and something draped on her head.

"Sheila, is that a tea towel?" I suppressed a laugh.

She ignored my question to say with dignity, "Cut them, please, three times," and, when I did, she set them out, one after another, peering at each one closely. She didn't speak for a long time.

"Sheila," I started to say, "Or should I call you something else when you're telling fortunes?"

"Sheila is fine," she said loftily.

"Where do you get tarot cards from?"

"These beauties," she tapped them, "come from the $2 shop in town."

"That doesn't sound very magical." I knew I sounded disappointed.

"These are *very* magical. Please cut them three times with your left hand, thinking of a question. But don't tell me what it is."

"But you already know," I protested, but cut the cards anyway.

She half-opened her eyes and lit her pipe. "Normally I'd have lit an incense stick for atmosphere. But you get the idea." She blew brown smoke out of the side of her mouth as she laid the cards, slap, slap, slap out on the wooden table in the shape of a fat cross.

We both leaned in to examine them closely. There was a man on a horse; a queen with flowing hair; a row of cups; two hairy men wielding swords. It made no sense at all.

"Interesting …" was all she said, drawing on her pipe.

I tapped my foot impatiently. There must be more. After a while I said, "What's there? What is it? There's a funny look on your face. What aren't you telling me? You can see something."

"That card there." She tapped a card with a picture of three gold swords. "That means a contest. The cup upside down means the end of a friendship. Or does it mean the beginning of something new? I'm a bit confused about that."

I didn't think clairvoyants were meant to be confused about such things, but I didn't say so. "Anything else?"

"Look here. That's a sexy man on your horizon …"

"But he's upside down," I wailed. "That can't be good."

"Not necessarily." Sheila's headband had slipped a little down over her right eye, pirate fashion. She rearranged it, deep in thought. "The fruits of your labour are yours for the taking. Be strong. Be brave. Be regular."

"Be regular?" It came out a squeak. Surely, cards weren't supposed to predict bowel movements?

"I'm just calling it as I see it," Sheila shot back. She settled more comfortably her chair, "What do you think? At $25, it's a bargain."

"Yep, a steal." I wiped my sticky, sweaty fingers on my dress and stood. "I'd better go. I should find Winona."

"Don't forget the brownies," and she handed me the container which now was half emptied by our emotional eating. "Or this," and Sheila tapped the book with the handle of her pipe.

I swiped up Sheila's copy of *Fifty Shades of Grey,* balanced it on the brownie container which I wedged under my chin and swung away down the path.

Chapter 7

The wind had dropped by then and the sun was warm across my back. I still felt chilled to the bone, though, imagining what had happened to Georgie Boy at the grubby hands, heaven forbid, of Mr McMuffin. I also couldn't help thinking about my handsome stranger. Or did the cards refer to Matt, like Sheila had hinted? Lost in thought, I didn't notice Jess, at first, coming from the other direction.

"Hey," I said. "Am I glad to see you!" and I did a little dance with my feet. She raised a pair of bright red Ray-Ban Wayfarers and watched my happy dance.

"Me, too." She hitched her canvas bag further up her shoulder, turned and fell into step with me. "I've been looking all over for you. Where have you been?"

I leaned my shoulder into hers, companionably. "Have you? Well, yay, here I am," and surreptitiously swapped the book with the container so it was on the bottom. I don't know why; Jess would laugh, maybe, at worst, but that was all. She's probably already seen the movie. I just didn't want to end up talking about sex, boys and, in particular, her brother.

"I've just come from Sheila, actually. You?"

"Nowhere, really. The beach for a bit and the games room."

That reminded me I was on duty. "Did you see Katie and Paris?"

"Yup. I also watched a couple of guys play pool." She pulled a face. "So, so bad and kinda boring, to be honest."

"Yeah, know what you mean. I've been watching the kids play volleyball. Well, fight over the ball, to be precise."

"With Sheila?"

"Nah, before I saw her. Did you know she's a clairvoyant now?"

Jess snorted through her nose. "She's crazy, that woman. What was she wearing?"

"A kaftan and a tea towel."

"For real?" Jess chewed on piece of hair and contemplated Sheila in napery. "Where are you heading?"

"Nowhere. What about you?"

"Same. But now that I've found you," Jess linked her arm through my elbow, "let's do something."

"Okay." I allowed myself to be dragged towards the picnic table we were supposed to meet at earlier where she hoisted herself onto the table, feet on the seat. I got up eagerly beside her. Jess always knew how to have fun. "Like, what?"

"Like, whatever," as she rummaged around her bag for her Coke Zero. She cracked it and put it down between us. "Here, take some of this. I need room for …" She kept rummaging until she pulled out a mini-bar-sized bottle of vodka, "… this."

"Whoa, Jess." I looked furtively left and right. "It's, like, three in the afternoon, someone might see us."

"Well, hide me so I can do this," and, while I covered her as best I could with my book and my body, she swiftly downed about one third of the Coke and tipped in the vodka.

"There," and with one dexterous throw, Jess dispensed with the little bottle in the basket bin nearby.

I stared at the can of Coke like it might explode.

"Well, are you going to drink it?" Jess said.

"Um, you first."

Jess snatched it up. Afterwards, she expelled air behind a dainty hand, giggled. It was my turn. I took it gingerly. It felt luke-warm in my hand and lighter than expected – Jess had drunk most of it. I took a small sip and another. It tasted sour like Vegemite so

I didn't mind that it was the last of it. I handed back the empty can.

"You look like you've just had your favourite celebrity voted off," she said. "Not a tasty drink."

"Sorry. Where did you get the vodka?"

"Mum's stash." Jess drank the dregs before scrunching up the can and sending it with a graceful lob into the same bin as the tinkling vodka bottle.

"Want me to take you to see Sheila?"

Jess wrinkled her nose.

"What's that for?" I said. "You love Sheila as much as me. "She taught us to knit, remember?"

Jess waved her hands around. "I know. I was just thinking about something less old-lady than haberdashery."

"Probably for the best," I said. "Sheila's not quite herself today, she's a bit upset about Stan's bird."

"What bird? And who is Stan?"

"You know, the guy with the long socks and sandals."

"Oh, that guy. He's one of Matt's weirdo friends. His bird just died, right? Matt told me. Sounds really cold."

I fanned myself with Sheila's book. The mention of Matt had raised my temperature by several degrees.

Jess noticed. "What's that you've got?"

"Huh?" I glanced at the book in my hand, "What? This? Nothing."

"Oh, yeah?" and she snatched it to read the title, "*Fifty Shades of Grey.* You've got to be kidding.

My mum read that book, but I didn't expect you to." She gave me respect fingers across her chest, but holding in laughter at the same time which kind of ruined my buzz.

"Look at these, they're all dog-eared. Is that you?"

"No!" I made a grab for it, Jess moving it out of my reach. I tried again, gave up. "Look, it's Sheila's." I didn't add that she'd been using as a way to spice up her love life with Stan.

"I don't know whether to be impressed or disgusted." She hitched her backside back onto the table, crossed her legs and began to swing them as she read aloud, in a deep sultry voice, about Christian and a handkerchief.

"Puleeze." She closed the book and dropped it on the table, her knotted bracelets sliding up and down. "You could always lend it to Winona and Matt."

She closed her eyes against the patchy sunlight swaying through the gum leaves. "I saw Winona just before. At the beach."

I don't know why, but that bugged me. I was on kid patrol so she could study, not get a tan. Several boogie boards on legs, balanced on the heads of invisible kids on their way to catch the last of the incoming tide, weaved past.

"Have you got a boyfriend?"

I glanced at Jess, but her eyes were closed.

"No," I said shortly. "You?"

"There's this guy in my class who I keep hooking up with, sorta friends with benefits. But I consider myself single. Matt hates him, anyway."

"Right."

"Is there someone you'd like to go all sado on?"

"Ewwww, that's so gross," which made us both lean forward laughing. When we'd calmed down, I said, "I saw Ben Forbes before," and I told Jess the story. She listened, her head tilted slightly to the left, and when I'd finished said, "Why don't we go find him, go back to your place? I reckon I could get more of those bottles."

"Better not. Winona's studying and there's the Terrible Two …" I trailed off. Jess nodded like she understood.

"Still, it must be pretty cool to be left here on your own."

"Sort of. It's also a lot of work." I was sure that sounded lame. But Jess didn't notice.

"What are you, like, getting paid for that?"

"Umm, $250."

"Shit. I know who to hit up for a loan later."

"Not getting it until after," I said hastily. "I'd better go. Check on Katy and Paris."

"There's going to be a beach party later. Not at Paradise. Around the next point, a bonfire at Sapphire. Wanna go?"

"Are you sure I'd be invited?"

Jess snorted. "It's not that sort of party. You just turn up."

I stood there, uncertain. Should I be making plans to go a party? I wanted to. Well, sort of. I hadn't been to many, more like gatherings. But tales of more notorious parties were rife. I shifted my weight around trying to decide.

"C'mon. It'll be fun. Everyone's going."

Did everyone include her brother? I chewed on my lip, thinking hard. Finally, I said, "I'll have to see what Winona's doing."

"She'll be going." Jess was matter of fact about that.

"What about Katy and Paris …?"

"They can come, too." Jess made it sound easy, a no-brainer.

I tipped an eyebrow. Did she know what she was suggesting? I held up a finger to put a stop to such madness. "You've forgotten the Twisties episode?" I referred to a time a few years back when Katy stuffed Twisties up the nostrils of one of the Morrison children, Charlie, I think, and held him down so a stray dog passing through the park could eat them because, as she said, "He looked so desperate and hungry."

Jess laughed. "And leaving them behind without supervision is better, how?"

She had a point. I imagined the consequences of those two in a house on wheels and filled with all our stuff and felt like fainting.

"You have to come. I need you." Jess entwined our fingers in an earnest display of her supreme neediness. "It's a beach party not a nightclub. They can't break anything and we won't let any dog near them. I'll watch them, too. Promise. I really want you to come."

Jess in beseeching mode is always very persuasive. I felt the reassuring warmth of her fingers in mine. Maybe, we could do it. I mean, how bad could they be with both of us – and Winona, if Jess was right and she was indeed going – keeping tabs on them.

I returned the squeeze of her hand. "You promise to help me."

Jess's nod was solemn. "I promise on our friendship bracelets that we buried together in the sand back in, umm, 2013 when we first met that I will help you control those monsters."

Monsters. It gave me the heebie jeebies. I made a sort of wry grinny grimace but nodded assent.

That wasn't enough, I could see. "Don't look so excited," said Jess and removed her hand. "It's not like I'm making you do this."

I reassured her. "It's just that I've not been to a beach party before." I didn't say that I'd not been allowed before. "It's going to be fun."

Jess squealed and flung herself off the picnic table, "Damn right it will be fun," jumping all over the place the way girls do, chanting, "Fricking fun, fun, fricking fun," eventually pulling herself together to say, "Right.

Great. Okay," making plans. "I'll come over beforehand, we can get dressed." She lost it again, started jumping around and chanting. So I did too – girly enthusiasm is kinda catchy like that – until she stopped, sucked in a breath and locked eyes with me and said, "Don't worry, it's going to be so awesome."

Spools of fluffy crimson colour had collected in the far west of the sky, a couple of kookaburras had taken line-out positions along a gum tree branch. It was getting late.

I picked up Sheila's book. "I'd better go find them before they do something stupid like pole dance all over the park's flag pole in front of Mrs Hitler. We'd be kicked out, for sure."

Jess pulled a sympathetic face but, I noticed, she didn't offer to help me with that.

Chapter 8

Winona was back by the time I got home, sitting with one tawny knee up in the banquet area, scooping out a tub of mango yoghurt and reading from *Wuthering Heights* as if she'd never been doing anything else but studying.

"Hi." I threw down the container of brownies and the book and sat down opposite, the beige vinyl seat making a hissing noise as the air left it.

"Oh, hi." Her eyes when they flickered my way were pistachio green. It was amazing how they did that: change with the light and seasons.

"Where have you been?" I said determined not to sound like Carolyn, but failing.

"Just around." Her reply was short, vague.

"Jess said you were at the beach." I made an effort to soften my voice. "How's the study?"

"It's going." Winona held up her open textbook.

"In case you were wondering, I've been seriously busy." I removed my Havaianas. "And now I've got blisters," hoping for a little sympathy, but getting none.

"I went over to Sheila's. She's having some sort of crisis, I think."

"Oh, yeah?"

"Well, she's acting a bit stranger than usual …" and I launched into tales of the dark arts; Georgie Boy going to the perch in the sky; sicko guys in dirty hoodies, when it struck me Winona wasn't even listening.

She put her nose close to me.

"What are you doing? Are you sniffing me?" drawing back, "Hey!" You are. Stop that."

"Have you been drinking?"

"No!"

Winona didn't believe me. "You have, too."

"I haven't!" then I remembered Jess's bottle of vodka and dropped my gaze.

"I ran into Jess and she had this can of Coke and a teeny weeny bottle of vodka, it was really cute, actually. It wasn't much, just a sip. Jess had way more. You're not going to tell Mum, are you?" I mean, it was unlikely with Winona, but, well, you never know.

Winona, with exaggerated care, folded down the page of her book and laid it on the table beside Sheila's contribution to my education. Had we not been distracted by my delinquency we might have both had a good laugh about that and how the themes of each one were similar even though they'd been written 200 years apart.

"First of all," said Winona, "as if I'd say anything to Carolyn …"

I waved my hand around. "I know, I know," to shut her up.

"Good," said Winona. A pause, then: "The thing is, you shouldn't be drinking."

"But I wasn't," I insisted. "I mean, it was only a sip." I didn't even like it.

"It can really mess with you," Winona went on. "Drinking is not the answer, believe me."

"And you'd know?" It came out with a note of resentment at her potential hypocrisy, but also in a hopeful way because I really wanted her to open up to me. She didn't. She kept lecturing.

"Sometimes so called 'friends' can make you do things. Bad things that you might not, you know, be able to handle."

I wondered what kinds of bad things she referred to and who she meant by friends. Did she mean Jess? Or was she talking about herself and Sinclair? It was hard to say and, anyway, I wasn't used to Winona like this. She was usually more chilled. And it sort of bugged me, to be honest, that she'd even brought up the issue of peer pressure because I was the Taylor most likely to resist it. I was into individuality. I wasn't a lemming, nor influenced by trends. I beat to my own drum, as she well knew.

"You *do* realise it's me you're talking to. Not Katy."

Winona said she knew that, but sometimes it can all feel a bit too much and you can get … reckless … and she said it like she was speaking from experience. So, of course, I asked again like a broken record what was going on with her and she just said, "It's complicated and I'd rather not talk about it," and returned to reading her book. This was just as infuriating as being scolded by her and brought me out in a prickly heat from top to toe.

I fanned myself with my fingers for a while but I could still smell the musty old caravan. It was like sitting inside one of Sinclair's socks after training. I hopped up to open a window and grab a cup of water. It tasted disgusting, like freezer, and I stuck out my tongue.

Winona caught it. "Really? I thought you said you were much older than Katy."

"I think you'll find I meant I was less easily led than Katy. But, anyway …" I put a cup of water near her pile of books. "It's disgusting, but good to stay hydrated while studying."

"Thanks."

And, all of a sudden, I felt sorry for her. She was under a lot of pressure with school and she'd broken up with Sinclair, who was probably the love of her life.

I just wished she confided in me like she used to. I missed that. Winona and I used to talk a lot about how we were feeling and what was going on with each of us. It used to make Jess envious. "I wish I had a sister to hang out with. I barely get a word out of Matt." I tried to offer her Katy, but, weirdly, she didn't accept.

"Hey, Winona?" I said staring at the golden crown of her bent head as she wrote notes in the margin of her novel.

"Hmmm."

"Have you heard about this beach party?"

"Hmmmm," not sounding interested.

"Jess said you're going."

"Going where?"

"To this party thing, on the beach." I waited a beat. "I'm thinking of going."

Her eyes flickered, interested now. She knew I hadn't been to many parties.

Winona lifted up a finger. "Wait. Let me get this straight. Maddy Taylor, the girl who won't embrace social media, who doesn't believe in sex before marriage and is terrified of kissing a boy in case she catches glandular fever, is contemplating going to a full-on beach party?"

"Well, yeah," I said, although, frankly, I didn't appreciate how she said it, making me sound like a freak, rather than an independent thinker which, by the way, the world needs more of.

"Sure." Winona gave a wicked little smirk. "Or is it that the smokin' hot Matt's going to be there?"

Hang on, Winona thought Matt was smokin' hot. Did that mean she was into him, after all? My heart flopped around like a dying fish before I found my voice.

"That's not it at all. Aren't you always telling me I need more life experience?"

"That's true." Winona raised a well-plucked brow. "And, anyway, it's not a crime to be hot for someone."

It is if your sister is into him. The thought popped into my head and I chased it away. She went on, "I always knew you liked Matt. After that time he rescued you on the rocks."

Jess and I had been sunbathing in the midday sun on the rocks the year before last when she'd dared me to dive into the hole in the rock between sets, and swim out to a yellow buoy bobbing about 100 metres offshore.

"I saw some little grommets doing it the other day, how hard can it be," laughed Jess when questioned on my ability to do it. I banished my doubts and stood on the rock shelf, my toes gripping the rough edge and my fingers pinching my nose shut while Jess counted through the waves, "One, two, three, go!" and I pencilled into the water just as a wave smashed onto the rock and sucked itself back out to sea taking me with it. It was dark beneath the surface and much colder than I'd expected. The shock forced my fingers from my nose and I immediately inhaled water, kicking furiously as I did. I banged my foot on a jagged submerged rock, grazing it badly but I didn't feel it straight away. I torpedoed for the surface but ended up further under and the lack of oxygen stung my lungs and I began to panic. I felt something tug me, a shark, and I screamed, sure I was about to die, swallowed even more water and prepared to be eaten, bones and all.

Instead, I was dragged up towards the fizzing light. When I broke the surface, with a whoosh, I gasped for air, confused and still thrashing, and heard someone say forcefully, "Stop doing that. You're kicking the crap outa me," and I realised that Matt was holding me in his arms. He rotated his hands so that they were under my armpits and pushed in an effort to get my head above water, but I kept slipping away from him. Still frightened, I flung my arms around his neck and tried to climb onto his back. Matt, who was probably already regretting his decision to rescue me, was forced under the waves himself. I attempted to stand on his head like it was a stepping stone. He dived down and came up behind me. "Would you get off me," when I squirmed around to reach for him again. He managed to get his arms under mine from behind and I felt him brace up to haul me out of the ocean.

I blinked into the blinding sunlight, water streaming from my hair and eyes, and saw Jess crouched over the edge of the rock platform, holding out her hands to pull me onto the rocks. I lay there dripping and gasping and limp. With a grunt, Matt pulled himself out of the water and turned me roughly onto my side so I could finish spitting out water. When I stopped coughing, I rolled onto my stomach and attempted to get up. He leaned back on his knees, watching me struggle for air, my swimming costume half off and my nose and eyes all red.

"You stupid idiot," he said eventually. He looked across to Jess who was hopping up and down nearby. "I suppose it was your idea."

"No way," she said, defiantly. "Well, Maddy wanted to do it, too."

I was too exhausted to disagree, and I suppose, in a way she was right. I stared at him, knowing I should probably thank him for saving my life but was transfixed by his heaving manly chest. I flopped on my back, panting and felt an emotion that was new and quite shocking in its intensity. Fuming about the fishing rod he'd had to drop in the water in order to dive in to save me, he shook his hair and droplets scattered all over me. I then realised I was bleeding profusely from my right foot and I felt like throwing up at the thought of losing all that O positive blood into the rock crevices. I must have whimpered because Matt sighed and picked up his towel. He wiped my snotty nose with the edge, then wrapped it gently around my foot and held it there until it stopped bleeding.

When I came out of my reverie, Winona was looking at me strangely. "Did you hear me? I think he's into you, too."

"Who?"

"Matt, you numpty."

I stared at her. "You really think that?"

Winona nodded.

"Nah, he can't be," I said, glancing away and then back to her. "Can he?"

Winona's eyes flickered briefly over my face, "Why not? You're a Taylor."

Yeah, just the wrong Taylor. I felt hysterical laughter rising up.

Winona said, "Why can't you accept that?"

"It's just that Jess thinks he's more into you than me."

Winona gave a snort of derision. "Course she'd say that."

"What does that mean?"

"Hmmm."

"Stop saying 'hmmm' all the time," I said. "It's driving me crazy."

"I think she can get a little bit jealous of you."

"Me!" I shook my head a little. Winona was nuts to think that. If Jess was jealous of anyone, it was of Winona not me.

Winona shrugged. "Whatever," as if she'd tried but given up on me, and ran a desultory finger around the edge of the empty yoghurt container.

I sighed. "What's the time?" thinking I should get onto dinner and other responsible stuff. I got up. The caravan swayed under my feet.

"Do you think Mum will call at seven, like she said she would?"

"I don't know, should we ask the fortune teller?"

So, Winona had been listening to me, after all.

"Ha ha ha," I said. "I know what we should ask her: are you getting back with Sinclair?"

Outside, I could hear kids laughing and chattering, the occasional parental shout of exasperation. A leaf blower started up. Birds began to make their afternoon noises.

She shot me an evil look. "No." But I couldn't tell if 'no' referred to getting back with Sinclair or asking our resident clairvoyant.

"What I want to know is: are you going to hook up with Matt Armstrong tonight?"

"Very funny," pretending that I hadn't already thought tons about exactly that.

She laughed and threw the empty yoghurt tub in the general direction of the sink. It missed.

"And while you're at it, could you ask Sheila where my bracelet is. I can't find it anywhere," she said.

I stared at her in surprise. First her bra and now her bracelet.

"It's gotta be here," I said. I figured it was either under a pile of Winona's crap, or attached to Paris's arm.

"Don't worry. I'll help you look for it," knowing how much she loved it.

I bustled the container into the bin I'd fashioned by hanging a plastic bag from the cupboard handle and went looking in drawers for a paper towel to wipe the yoghurt drops from the floor.

"I'm thinking of moving my stuff into Mum's room," she said. "It'll probably turn up then."

I had begun to scrabble around for my thongs. "Okay," without lifting my head.

She began to move her bag, pillow, towel and books from the annexe to the main bedroom, spreading warm air scented with coconut as she swished to and fro.

Ahh! I spied my thongs under the edge of the seat closest to the bedroom and sank my left cheek onto the sticky vinyl floor to reach for them with an extended arm. Winona saw me struggling and kicked them towards me.

"Thanks," I said and sat back on my haunches to arrange them side by side ready for putting on.

"You don't mind, do you?" she said.

"Nope," I said. I thought about my blisters and pushed the instruments of torture back under the table.

"I'm going to turn on the barbecue then go find the girls."

At the door, I turned and called out, "Hey."

"What?" Winona reappeared from the bedroom, tying up her hair with a black band.

"What's a hook-up? I mean, I know what it is. But, specifically, what is it exactly?"

She leaned a shoulder against the concertina door.

"It's whatever you want it to be."

"So, like, kissing and stuff ..."

"Yeah ... and sex."

"But mostly kissing, right?"

"Umm, well, mostly sex."

"No way." I was shocked.

Winona, nodded, "'Fraid so. Heard of the term 'Netflix and chill?' Sex."

Hang on a minute. Chilling in front of Netflix didn't mean chilling in front of Netflix? My head began to reel and I squeezed my eyes shut as a few prior conversations with friends began to make more sense, especially them cackling. When I opened them, Winona had disappeared again.

"Why the hell is everything about sex?" I called out. "What happened to love?"

"You make like sex is a bad thing," her voice coming from the bedroom, "It's not. It's gorgeous, like swimming naked in warm water."

"Ewww." The thought of me, Winona or anyone doing *it* gave me prickles all over. I mean, I knew my sister had probably had sex with Sinclair, but I didn't have to dwell on it. Winona reappeared.

"Listen, Ms Hearts and Flowers, you're going to have to let go sometime."

I crossed my arms. "No way, not until I'm in love."

"What's love got to do with it?" Winona laughed but I didn't like the way it didn't quite make it to her eyes.

"But, but … you and Sinclair loved … love … each other, don't you?"

She didn't answer. Instead she pushed passed me. "I'm going to have a shower."

Chapter 9

I stood at the window and saw Winona, so assured, yet somehow so fragile, too, with her tiny shell-shaped ears and halo of hair, drift along the path between the nylon tents towards the main building. Funny how you can live with someone, share their DNA, cry with them over *The Lion King* – okay, so it was just me crying – and still not understand them at all.

My attention became caught by the Richardson baby capering around starkers, his mother cooing, "Time for din dins, darling."

Was it that late already? I'd better get moving.

The barbecue was down the side of the caravan on a dark strip of patchy grass near the recycling bins. I shivered and wrinkled my nose at the garbagy smell and raised the rusty lid, nearly gagging at the dried fat and bits of burnt onion. Some people were disgusting. I held my hand across my mouth and, with a scrap of newspaper I dug out of the recycling bin, tried to clean the grill. I gave up, threw the dirty newspaper back into the bin, twiddled the gas bottle valve, turned the knob hard and clicked the red button, whoosh. Instantly, the white grease disappeared into a slick puddle. I stood there, mesmerised by the chemistry of heat, until I had the distinct sensation of being examined. I shivered. It was cold. My shoulders tightened. I glanced left and right and, eventually, up. Two pairs of beady, greedy eyes stared boldly back – kookaburras, after some easy dinner.

Holy crapola, they had me going. I tipped the plate of sausages onto the grill and hustled back around to the front of the caravan.

I stopped outside the doorway, the flap against my cheek. I had the distinct impression someone was inside. Winona back from her shower already? I doubted it. She took forever. Katy? If it was, it was about time. But somehow it didn't feel like the girls. What if it was someone else? Someone wearing a hoodie who'd already stolen a valuable bracelet and had returned to the scene of the crime looking for more loot or our emergency money. I tiptoed forward and raised the flap so quietly I could hear the blood in my ears.

The annexe was empty. Not a hoodie clad figure in sight. I breathed deeply, in and out. Just then something touched my shoulder and I nearly jumped out of my skin. I flung myself around and stared into the square perspiring face of Mrs Richardson, a dishcloth over a shoulder and a benign inquiring look on her face.

"Are you okay, dear?"

I nodded, speechless, my heart still going bang, bang, bang, 100 kilometres an hour, the tongs still raised above my head. Slowly, I lowered them.

"No, I'm fine," I managed to say, "Thanks."

Mrs Richardson's hand fluttered to an imaginary strand of pearls at her neck. "I just wanted to see if there was anything you needed. I know you girls are staying here for a few days on your own. Your mother came and told me."

"No, we're good. But thanks," I said. No point in mentioning my lively imagination or those devilish kookaburras. I waited for Mrs Richardson to leave, but she kept standing there.

"I just wanted you to know that, um, a fellow has been seen creeping around the park. So," her eyes took in my bare legs and chest, "Be careful."

"Sure thing, Mrs Richardson." I stepped backwards feeling the canvas flap on my back. "Umm, if that's all, I'm going to, er, get back to making dinner."

I threw the tongs into the sink and turned around. And nearly had another heart attack at the sight of

Jess sitting at the banquet seat, reading a book. She was dressed in skinny jeans, a flannel shirt – Matt's? – over a bandeau, her hair half up and half out.

"Oh, hey," she said, sounding as if she lived here.

"Freaking hell, Jess. What are you doing here?"

"I thought we'd decided we'd go to the party together. By the way," her sweeping hand took in all of Winona's mess on the table and in the bedroom. "Love what you've done to the place."

"Sorry. We've been looking for Winona's bracelet," though why I was apologising to Jess, I didn't know. I shook my head, feeling cross.

"Well, now you're here, you might as well help with dinner."

"Me?"

"Make a salad, at least." I had got out the onions and some carrots and was looking for the breadboard and a knife.

"Like, how?"

I handed her the onions and a knife. "Chop these."

"Ewww, no way. I hate the smell of onion," but she began to peel one.

"Has Winona really lost her bracelet. That's bad. Is it expensive?"

"Tiffany," I said. "From Dad."

"I thought they were real diamonds," said Jess. "You should put up a notice in the office. Offer a reward or something."

"Maybe." I tried to peel carrots with a plastic peeler left over from the Dark Ages. Or maybe I could just go through Paris's things … was I failing in my duty if I hadn't seen the girls in hours? But it was so peaceful without them.

"Where's Winona?" Jess said.

"Shower." I rattled drawers and cupboards looking for a bowl.

"Getting ready for tonight?" Jess guessed. She began to cut the onions into quarters, "What are you wearing?"

"Jeans. No, not that way." I made a grab for the knife and the onions. "Give it to me."

Jess let them go, grinning.

"Here." I threw over the tongs. "Get the sausages."

Jess rested her chin on her hand. "In a minute. Matt's going, you know. Maybe he and Winona, you know …"

"Hook-up?"

"Who's going to hook-up?" Katy said loudly, clattering into the caravan.

"None of your business," I said. "Not you, that's for sure."

"That's what you think," Paris said, appearing beside Katy. "Jess! Thanks for that tan tip."

I glared at Jess. "What tip?" and then to Katy, "And what the hell time do you call this?"

"And what do you call this?" she countered, holding out a plate of charred remains.

Oh crap. The sausages. Burnt into lumps of charcoal.

"Just give them bread and water," Jess said, grinning. "As punishment for being late."

"That's basically what they had for lunch." I flopped onto the banquet, deflated. I'd forgotten the barbecue, hadn't covered the food groups, was scared of kookaburras and parties and, basically, everything. I couldn't even take care of my little sister and her friend. I blew out air which sent my fringe into orbit.

"Where have you been?"

"Living our lives to the max," said Paris, opening up the fridge, grabbing a can of lemonade and pouring it into two glasses, one for her, one for Katy. She slid in beside Katy and put a sausage into her cup and stirred it around. The girls both laughed. "You should see the looks on your faces," Katy said. "Heard from Carolyn yet?"

"Not yet," I said, not bothering to correct her for her use of Mum's name. "I'm going to the office in a minute to wait for her call."

"Could you buy some sauce while you're there," said Katy, licking her fingers. "Hide the burnt taste of these."

"Could you be more specific about how you've been living your lives," I said, handing over a wodge of paper towels.

"First we played volleyball and won." Katy and Paris high fived one another. "And then we went in the pool. We played Marco Polo which we lost, but that was because Toby cheated. Then we worked on our tan the way Jess showed us. See?" Katy flashed her reddened back at me. "No bikini line."

I saw. "Topless! How many times do I have to remind you? You're only *13*."

Katy took another bite, chewed for a moment, unfazed, and swallowed, "She says this party at Sapphire's going to be huge, don't you Jess? So, we're going, right?"

"Course you are," said Jess. Katy glanced in my direction checking to see if I planned to contradict Jess. I didn't.

"Yes!" Katy and Paris locked eyes.

Winona returned from the shower looking damp but radiant, a towel across her shoulders. She used an edge to rub her ears.

"What are you two looking so smug about?" she said.

"Jess said we're going to this party tonight. What are we going to wear?"

Winona gave Jess a nod hello. "Don't care what you wear," she said. "You're only going if you behave. Now buzz off. I want to talk to Maddy. Excuse us, Jess." Winona pulled me into her room, shutting the concertina door behind her. "What is she doing here?"

"Jess? She just arrived. Wants to go with us to the party, I think." I was faintly puzzled. Wanting to hang out here wasn't a crime.

"Okay, fine. I'm not even sure if I'm going," Winona hissed.

"Please, please, pretty please." I so didn't want to go to the party without her.

"Got HSC in less than a month."

"I know," but I kept staring at her pleadingly.

"Oh, okay, what the hell. I'll probably go crazy otherwise." Winona threw her damp towel on the bed. "Only on one condition."

I bounced down on the bed. "What's that?"

"You make an effort to look good and try to have an open mind."

"Of course," I said. "I always do."

"No, you don't. Like tonight, you're probably going to wear jeans, a size 12 black T-shirt and a beanie. Am I right?"

"Yep, pretty much." What was wrong with being *comfortable*?

Winona reached in a cupboard and held up a short dress. "Wear this."

"No, thanks. I'll be cold. And my legs are too pale."

"Haven't you heard of fake-tan?"

I shook my head. I could be stubborn.

"Okay then, what about this?" holding up a floaty top.

"Can I wear it with a cardi?" I said.

"Only if you don't call it a cardi."

"What if no one talks to me?"

"Of course, someone's going to talk to you," and when I raised a doubtful brow, "Me, for one."

"Someone other than a blood relative." I buried my face in my hands. "Bluck, ugguhuggg," as the reality of going to a party hit me. "Why does it matter so much? Mum says I'm expressing myself, the way I dress."

"You can express yourself any way you like, just not in your pyjamas at a party." Winona laid a skirt and top combination on the bed. "Weren't you the one printing out the perfect resort wardrobe before, and asking all those questions about sex?"

I couldn't argue. It was true. I wanted to impress Matt. But what if he only had eyes for Winona? My stomach clenched.

"I'm not going to this party. I don't want to." I collapsed back on the bed. "I'll just do something dorky and be laughed at if I go."

"Oh, Maddy." It was Winona's turn to sigh. "No one's laughing at you. Or if they do, it's because you're funny." She added a belt to the outfit on the bed.

"You could wear this with your Converses and a cardigan. Why don't we take off that hideous black polish, it's chipped anyway, and I'll paint your nails something pretty."

"Boys. They just don't get me," I wailed, as she bent over my nails.

"Only one needs to get you."

Yeah, but the *one* I had in mind didn't seem to get me at all.

Winona, when she glimpsed my doleful expression, said in an attempt to reassure me, "Don't worry so much. It's a party, not a test." She applied the polish to my fingernails and, bending, to her own toe-nails. "There," she pronounced satisfied and screwed the lid back on the polish.

What would I do without Winona, I asked myself, watching as my sister blew carefully on my nails she'd just painted a soft orange. I loved my mum, don't get me wrong, but Winona was the one who always made me feel understood.

When Mum rang, I should probably tell her about the party and the missing bracelet and everything.

Chapter 10

In the end, I didn't tell Mum anything. The conversation I had with her was altogether unsatisfactory, mostly because, once she ascertained that we were all alive and well, she began to have multiple discussions with other people in the room. Finally, she said, "I'd better go, honey. Things are very hectic here. Sleep well. I'll call you this time tomorrow," and she was gone.

"I love you," I said to the empty air and walked slowly back to the caravan to get dressed for the party in the clothes Winona had set out for me.

The full moon hung low and heavy over our shoulders and the night wind bit into our cheeks and tore words from our mouths as we made our way around the point to Sapphire. When we reached the corner, the wind dropped away and the ocean flattened itself out like a bedspread but we remained silent, our feet making deep indents in the heavy sand.

Jess, Katy and Paris began to giggle, but I was too nervous and my throat was dry. Beside me, Winona removed her sandals to make walking easier. I was glad to be wearing sneakers. When I looked behind me to see how far we'd come, I saw their distinctive pattern stamped into the sheet of sand trailing behind.

I glanced at the girls, each wearing self-satisfied expressions and one of Paris's feathered drop earrings, the cloying strawberry scent of their lip gloss wafting behind them as they tore ahead of us, stopping every 30 seconds to hug one another.

Winona, who had switched to the red floral dress and a denim jacket, was looking luminous. Though she had insisted on eyeliner for me, nearly poking out my eye as she applied it, her own face was bare of make-up. I tried not to rub mine off as we trailed along after the girls.

When I looked ahead I could see the bonfire shooting sparks at the sky and heard screaming laughter. *Arrest Me* blared from speakers rigged up on a pile of upturned milk crates. As we drew closer, I made out two eskies wedged between them, lids up, and a group of boys clowning around beside beer cans already in their hands.

A big guy with boardshorts slung so low on his hips I could make out the deep V of his stomach saw us first and shouted, "Winona. Can I get you a drink?"

"'Sup?"

"Hey, babe."

Jess and I were jostled sideways as one boy after another, all of them strangers to me, made passes for Winona. In the darkness, I lost sight of Jess, but managed to grab Katy and Paris, whose normally bug eyes were practically on stalks. One guy failing to make any impression on Winona switched his attention to Katy, giving her the once over with a lascivious air.

"Don't even think about it?" I warned, pushing closer and staring until he dropped his gaze and shambled further away.

"Ah, can I get you girls a Red Bull or something?" It was Charlie Tugwell, his hair damply combed from his face, freckles stoked up and almost livid by the fire.

"They'll have Coke Zeros, thanks," I said firmly, shushing Katy with a hand when she began to protest that she'd really prefer a Red Bull. It was self-preservation, pure and simple, for I knew if I let them drink Red Bulls, I'd never be able to control them. Katy and Paris sculled two Cokes and, mad on sugar highs, whooped it into the darkness to a spot with a tumbling down pipe where they produced an energetic show for the Tugwells, the Morrisons and Alex Gordon and, when they grew tired of that, a running race up and down the beach. I kept an eye on them as I stood beside Winona, sipping from a bottle handed to me, remembering Winona's warning, and tried too hard not to wait for Matt.

"Hey, you're the girl from the beach," said a guy close to my ear. I jumped, startled, and glanced at Winona to make sure that he wasn't in fact talking to her. She was doing her best, I noticed, to look impressed at some guy's tattoos without yawning.

"Remember me?" he said, making room beside me. Invisible fingers squeezed at my heart as I realised that I did: the guy from the beach with the dog.

"I'm Malcolm," putting a hand across his heart as if he was telling the whole truth and nothing but. "But my mates call me Mal. You can, too."

I thought about Georgie Boy and didn't want to answer. But I had an image of Barney, and the way his tongue lolled about during his epileptic-like fit on the sand earlier and I felt confused. Maybe, I was wrong about him. A guy with a dog like Barney couldn't possibly twist a little bird's neck with his fingers.

"Madison," I said.

"Hi, Madison." He held out his hand.

His nails were bitten to the quick and, reluctantly, I shook it. He held mine a moment too long. I pulled it away. He wasn't offended, just let me go, "And are youse staying at Sapphire or Paradise?"

"Paradise," I took a biggish gulp of my drink. It was cold and sweet and slid down easily.

"The girls are always hot at Paradise," he said, looking appreciatively, first at me and then at Winona, "if you get my meaning."

Unfortunately, I did and looked away, embarrassed at the lame pick-up line. He half grinned, sheepishly, but slyly too, pretty sure he'd just about nailed it – and me, and went on, "I could get you 'nother."

"Sure," I said just to be rid of him. While he was gone, I finished the one I had and tuned in to the conversation Winona was having about tattoos. *Teenage Dream* was playing and the irony didn't go unnoticed by me.

"This one took about three hours and hurt like hell," said a Zen surfer with hair so bleached from the sun it almost glowed in the moonlight, "because of the colours I chose. The deeper the colour and more shading, the longer the needle pokes you. I nearly passed out."

Winona glanced at the arm, looked away. "Wow."

"I could teach you to surf. I've got a spare Springer."

"What's that?" said Winona, interested in spite of herself.

The guy sensed his luck might have changed. "It's a short wetsuit."

"I don't have to wee in it, do I?"

"Oh, babe." The guy hung his head. He couldn't imagine this goddess actually performing human bodily functions. I nearly laughed out loud. She could fart for Australia.

Mal returned with my drink, his wide brown thongs flicking sand all over the place, reddish hair flopping over his narrow eager face. I kept my expression bland, and my head turned slightly away. Out of the corner of an eye I saw him shove a bit to get himself into place beside me. I took the drink without thanks. It was another Vodka Cruiser; he'd already courteously opened it. I took a gulp, doing my best to ignore him. Winona leaned in to me. "Watch it. Those drinks can sneak up on you."

"Yeah, yeah," I said. Mal took this as a sign of encouragement. He said, peering up at the sky and scratching his stomach with a lazy hand, "Good night for pig shootin'"

I felt my eyes goggle. Shooting? Really? I took another gulp.

"What about you? Ever been shootin'?"

"Yep, oh yeah, I go all the time." I inched away, ever so slightly. He might not be the bird killer, but this guy was definitely a sandwich short of a picnic, with his ergonomic shoes and talk about killing pigs.

"Really?"

"No!" Couldn't he tell I was being sarcastic?

I pointed to myself "Me, pacifist." A statement that had an air of finality about it, a full stop, end of story, good bye. But Mal, it seemed, didn't see it that way. He took another sip of his drink, "Want to come for a walk?" and thrust out his hips slightly so there was no mistaking his meaning.

"Nope, but thank you for your lovely offer." I smiled sweetly before shutting my lips with a snap.

His face fell. I could almost see the cogs of his brain going, hey what just happened? I thought we were getting along. Where's my payment for that drink I fetched? I took another mouthful of drink, rolling it around on my tongue, thinking, someone ought to shoot him, in the arse, ha!, see how he likes it. Through the upturned glass bottle, I watched Mal gather himself up, shake his head, mutter something under his breath and slouch away. Good riddance. I saluted myself and drank from the bottle. Before I knew it, I'd almost finished it. Whoa. What did Winona say? Take it easy with these drinks. Quickly I bent down and tipped out the remains into the sand.

Now what? The air twined itself around my legs like a cat. I tipped my head back to peer at the stars. They were so bright, so radiant, so far away. My perspective shifted so that I was looking down at them. I was falling, falling into them. The world, then, righted itself and I found myself focusing on the faces around me, none of them I recognised. Probably residents of Sapphire Park, the next holiday spot around from us. I felt separate from it, like I was inside a clear but protective bubble. Even Miley Cyrus's throaty voice had dulled to a low hum. Flames from the fire gushed up as someone tossed on a stream of white spirits. The crowd roared approval. It sounded like they were underwater. I shivered. It was cold. I unslung my cardigan and put it on.

This was exactly why I didn't go to parties. The music was crap and I was no good at flirting. The only guys I could attract were creeps. I patted down my hair. The salty air had made it frizzy. A piece of shell blew into my eye and it began to water. I rubbed too hard, smearing mascara over my face. And, as it turned out, beach parties were the worst.

When I next looked up it was at Jessica. "I found you," she said and positioned herself beside me to take in the party. She held the neck of a beer loosely between two fingers and swigged from it, her eyes swivelling from the fire to the boys howling near the esky and, finally, back to me.

"What are you drinking?"

I held out my empty bottle. "Cruiser."

Jess lifted my bottle to her eye, saw it was empty and turned it up upside down and shook it. "Way to go, girlfriend."

I didn't bother to tell her that it was empty because I'd poured the rest of it away. Even so, I felt weird. Was this what being drunk was like? Jess, seemingly unaware of my discomfort said, "I've been talking to Ben and a friend of his. They want to take us for a walk."

A walk? I wiped my mouth with the back of my hand. That could be hard since I no longer had feeling in my toes. Jess kept talking. "They're over there. No, don't look. They're coming over." Jess nudged me and waved at them. She said under her breath to me, "Check Ben out. Is he cute or what?"

"Sure," I said, wondering if Ben would say anything about us meeting up at the kiosk. My mouth felt dry. I had trouble swallowing.

"Whatever you do, stay cool." Jess rearranged her hair over her shoulders and produced a bored expression. I feigned great interest in my nails so I didn't have to see their approach. I only looked up when they were standing right in front of us.

"Hi."

"Oh, hi," I said as if I was surprised to see them.

"Hi, Maddy. It's been a while." Ben gave me an insider's grin.

"Yep, ages." I smiled back, I couldn't help myself. Jess was right, he *was* pretty cute. Jess gripped the fleshy part of my forearm and gave it a pinch, saying over the top with a beguiling smile, "Are you having a good time?"

Ben exchanged looks with his friend. "We are now, aren't we Dan?"

"Definitely." Dan's head went up and down emphatically. Like Ben, the buttons of his flannel shirt weren't done up over his T-shirt and his tight trousers were slung low. It seemed boys had a uniform, too.

"Let me get you girls a drink," Ben said, a smile still playing around the corners of his mouth, and in his eyes, too, as they settled on me for one second, two seconds. This made me prickle with pleasure until I felt Jess stiffen, heard her breath catch as she noticed this. But by the time my eyes swivelled to her face, I could only detect indifference as she took a final pull from her drink and held it up. "I'll have this again." He took it, and looked my way questioningly. I shook my head. "No thanks."

Chapter 11

Ben trotted back with beers that he'd already opened, handing them out and, winking as he gave me one, "You said no, but I got you one anyway."

"Er, thanks, but I don't think I like beer," but took it.

He wasn't really listening, busy as he was with something tucked into his top pocket.

"Wait till you see what I've got." He held up a giant uneven cigarette, saying as he lit it, "My brothers swear by this gear."

As the sweet faintly nauseous smoke wrapped around me, I felt my pulse quicken. Cannabis. Marijuana. Dope. I'd never seen it smoked before.

"You dog, you," grinned Dan, pulling hard when it was his turn so that the head fizzed in the dark like fireflies. He held his breath, the joint pinched between two fingers, letting smoke drizzle, dragon-like, through his nose before passing it along to Jess.

Holding my beer and watching Jess take a toke, she doing it with all the assurance of a seasoned dope smoker, I wondered at the audacity of smoking drugs in the middle of a party. Behind me Ed Sheeran's *Shape of You* played. I nodded along. The music, at least, was better. I could hear chatter from those sprawled in front of the fire, occasional screams as timber cracked in the heat.

"Maddy, go on, take it." Jess held the joint out for me. I stared at it, flaming in the darkness, wondering what I would do? Was this a life experience or the gateway to drug addiction?

"It won't bite, you know." Jess put it between my fingers.

"I know," I said crossly. I wished Jess wouldn't look at me like that. I took a tentative puff, aware of both boys. The smoke rasped through my nostrils, tickled the back of my throat. Some of it made it into my lungs, which stung. I coughed a few times and handed the joint back to Ben.

He took it, finished it, and saying, as he buried the paper end in the sand, "It's going off back there," nodding behind him and putting his mouth against the edge of beer bottle's rim. Beneath the magnification of the glass his lips looked enormous, like two slugs.

I wished I didn't feel so strange. Take it easy, Winona had said. I held my beer up to check it out in the crinkly light of the fire and took another tentative sip. It still tasted bitter and some of it spilled. I wiped my mouth, thinking, ha ha ha I have a drinking as well as a drug problem.

The party swirled around and pressed against us, trying to get into our tight circle, make a conga line of it. Standing upright and independent took some effort.

The words of a song came into my head, loud and clear as if they were being piped directly into my ears, not through speakers; a song just for me. I listened intently to the words, trying to figure out what they meant about a loaded gun, and a battle drum, and no time to fall apart.

"Are you feeling all right?" Jess loomed in, looking worried – or annoyed; it was difficult to tell.

"Course. I don't even like this song." I tipped my head on its side and banged my ear so that notes spilled out onto the sand. Scattered about, they resembled the tiles from a Scrabble set. I almost didn't want to bury them. But I had to. It was the only way to get rid of the music. I dropped to my knees and scratched about in the sand.

'What are you doing?" Jess slithered to her knees beside me, puzzled, sure, but getting impatient, too. I lifted up my shoulders extravagantly.

"Digging a hole to put the song in," I said.

"What song? What are you talking about?" Ben said. He had finished his drink and threw the bottle deep into the whirling blackness. Jess cast a look back at the two boys standing over us and twirled her finger around her ear, the universal sign for cuckoo.

"Whatever she's on, I want it. She's priceless." Dan ogled with interest, his arms crossed, as I scattered sand. "What's she doing now?"

"Stop that." Jess pulled me up by my arm. I dusted off my hands.

"Where are we going?"

"Getting away from here," she said. "I don't want my brother to see us like this."

I pulled away. "I need to check up on Katy."

But the boys nodded. They were up for a bit of privacy, sure, why not? Good to get some distance from the crowd. The dunes looked like the place to head; somewhere romantic and quiet. Jess started walking, steering me in front of her with two arms. Dan, on the other side of Ben, was trying to get a better look at me.

"You look familiar. How do I know you?"

"Do you know Winona?" Jessica said.

"Duh," he said. Everybody knew Winona.

"Well, Maddy's her sister," Jess said.

This impressed Dan. He looked me up and down with his head slightly to the side. "I heard she had a sister."

I waved him away, feeling like a freak, a sideshow. Ben draped his arm around my shoulders, a display of ownership.

Jess skipped out in front. "Did you know I can tie up a cherry stalk with my tongue and my hands behind my back?"

"Really?" Dan buried his hands into his pockets, his eyes finally on Jess. "What else can you do with your tongue?"

"Wait and see." Jess giggled and pushed his arm.

"I don't feel very well," I said quietly to Jess.

"Pull yourself together. Dan is hot and he's definitely into me. You're not going to spoil it."

What about Jess's infatuation with Ben? I pulled myself up straight, an invisible cord running through my spine like a puppet. My beer flipped upside down and amber fluid ran down the side of my leg.

Whoopsies. I hoisted the bottle, gave my sneakers a good shake and declared that I was good to go. All I really longed to do was to sink down into soft sand, pull down the sky and curl up beneath it, a star patterned doona, to take a nap.

"Let's stop here," said Dan and Ben, together, taking stock of the situation, measuring, with keen eyes, the distance we were from the party and how far we still had to go to make it to the sand dunes and recognising futility when they saw it. The sand was cold and we sat in a daisy chain of entwined limbs to keep warm. I could feel the heat of Ben's knee radiating through the skin beneath my slithery skirt. Rheumy moonlight made it impossible to see facial expressions, just holes for eyes and holes where mouths were supposed to be. My skin went all fluttery like I'd swallowed a hive of bumble bees.

I became aware of Ben's knee, jiggling up and down against my own. I dared myself to glance his way. He took my hand and held it in the dark.

Jessica gave us a filthy look, got up and climbed into Dan's lap, draping her arms about his neck and nuzzling his ear. Eventually, with a look angled towards Ben, Dan said that he and Jess were going to check out the dunes. I tried to tell Jess that they were so far away, like a billion steps. She shook her head. She was up for it. She arched a kink out of her back and stretched out her arm for Dan's hand. Together they wandered up the beach, Jess on tiptoes and Dan lightly slapping her backside whenever it was aimed at him.

It was awkward left behind with Ben. I had trouble seeing him properly; he listed slightly to the right. Or was it me? I scrunched up my eyes. Tight waves crashed rhythmically on the shore and the moon made a grab for the outgoing tide. I let my bottle of beer tip over and let the last of the brown fluid drain away. I wiggled my toes inside my sneakers, trying to get the feeling back, doing the same with my fingers.

Ben moved closer, put his arm across my shoulder and murmured, "Cold?" I jumped. I'd forgotten he was there.

"I guess," I said slowly, staring down at his hand that had ended up dangling over my left breast. Okaay. This is cool. I'm cool. He leaned in and kissed me on the mouth. I kissed back, politely at first. His breath was warm and lemony, not unpleasant, and I didn't mind when he kept his lips on mine, pressing harder and opening a little. I could feel the point of his tongue at my teeth. My lips sank open and he pushed his tongue in further. Whoa, I didn't sign up for that. Or did I? I gasped, or tried to, but found I couldn't breathe. I jerked my head back, my jaw clenched.

"Fucking hell," he said, leaping up in surprise and wiping his mouth. "Shit. Did you just bite me?" I put my hand over my mouth, horrified. Did I? God, I think I did. "I'm sorry," I gasped. "I think it was a reflex; a survival mechanism."

He shook his head in disbelief. "You're kidding me."

He put out his tongue, and gingerly pressed his finger to it. It came away bloodied.

"You bloody well did. You bloody well bit me." He clambered up, snatched at his drink, slapped sand from his mustard coloured jeans. "You're a bloody lunatic, a tease."

What did that mean? I watched the darkness monster swallow him up. Wait, I felt like calling out, give me another chance. I'll do better. It was a surprise, is all. I snuck a glance towards the dunes, hoping Jess hadn't witnessed my humiliation, but all I could see was nothing.

I was alone. My head felt soggy like Weet-Bix left too long in milk. I shook it, a mistake. It was cold and the sand felt like a block of ice but I lay back and closed my eyes. The earth bucked. I sat up quickly. What was wrong with me? I pressed my cheeks with my fingers, I couldn't feel them. Did that mean they weren't there?

I heard footsteps, someone panting with exertion.

"Jess?" My voice wavered in the dark.

"No, it's me." Winona stood over me, bending a little to see if I was laughing or crying, happy or sad, or unconscious. I stared up at her, please, please, help me. But it wouldn't come out. She held out her hand.

"Come on, get up," and tried to heft me up. I was too heavy for her and I fell back down.

"It's hopeless. I'm hopeless. I bit Ben's tongue. A song tried to brainwash me. I can't move. My cheeks are numb and I might have wet my pants." At that I began to cry, big wobbly tears that fell down my numb cheeks.

"You're drunk. What did I say about those Cruisers?"

"But I only had one and … and … about that much." I held up my finger to illustrate, and then used it to wipe across my snotty nose. I wouldn't mention the other thing.

"Looks like one's enough for you," Winona said, but kindly.

"Leave me here. Just dig me a hole and bury me."

"Where are your friends?" Winona looked about her.

"They left me."

Winona could see that it was futile to try to carry me. She lowered herself beside me, clasped her knees with one arm, and put her other around my shoulders. I leaned into her.

"How did you even find me?"

"Matt saw you go off from the party with Jess and those two guys. He was worried and came and got me and went to find Jess."

I rubbed my eyes, lifted my face up to Winona.

"How do I look? I bet I look gross. Has my mascara come off?"

"You look like a panda."

"But they're cute, right?"

"Only to another panda."

"I feel weird." I shook my head. "If drinking does this, I don't know why anybody would do it. I don't suppose you've got Katy and Paris with you?" My voice trailed off. Great babysitter I turned out to be.

"Yeah, Matt's been keeping an eye on them. He only left them to follow you and Jess."

She hoisted herself up. "Come on. We've got to get you home."

I grasped her outstretched tapered hand and tried to get up. The world tripped over again. And again.

"Oh, hey. Can you help me?" I heard Winona say to someone. The next thing I knew, strong arms had taken me under my arms and hauled me up. I leaned heavily against a strong chest with a warm beating heart. I nuzzled in. The T-shirt felt rough beneath my cheek, the scent of wood and smoke and something else familiar – citrusy aftershave? – tickled my nose. Where had I smelled that before?

"I'm worried. She's acting weird. Probably drunk. She's not used to drinking." Winona's voice, but she wasn't talking to me.

"Let's get her walking. The fresh air might straighten her up," the deep voice was familiar. It was Matt Armstrong.

I burrowed my face in his shoulder, the one with the arm trying to hold me up. He just grunted. It seems I was heavier than I appeared.

His other hand, the one on my ribcage, was warm. I felt myself slide down his stomach to where his untucked T-shirt met his jeans. I scrabbled with my hands trying to stay upright. While I was there, I attempted to peek down his pants.

"Do you, like, have a pair of red superhero Speedos under those jeans?"

"Stop that," he said, pushing my hand away.

"What did she say?" Winona said anxiously. "Is she making sense yet?"

"Nope."

Winona tried to put Matt's jacket around my shoulders. It fell off. Winona tried again. It fell off again so she draped it over her own shoulders, her hair half caught beneath it, looking for all the world like she was hailing a cab outside a nightclub.

"Keep walking, sweetheart," Matt muttered.

"Don't sweetheart me," I muttered, but obediently I started up again. "You're not a superhero. You're just bossy."

"Did she just call you a superhero?" Winona found a stick of gum in his jacket pocket and offered it around.

"Yep," he said over my head.

"Which one?"

"She wasn't specific," he said spitting out strands of my hair getting caught in his mouth. "Hopefully not the Incredible Hulk. Green isn't my colour."

"What's wrong with Maddy?" Katy and Paris crowded up, peering closely at my face. "She's drunk, isn't she? I knew it!"

"She is not," Winona said. "Give her space."

"She looks drunk as a skunk," said Katy. "Where's Jess? I bet she's the same."

"Yeah," Winona turned to Matt, "What does Jess look like?"

"Better than this, but she's used to it." Matt patted the frizz down on my hair. Katy and Paris turned their attention to him. "Hey, you're Jess's brother," said Katy and, in a loud whisper to Paris, "That's the guy who Maddy likes but who likes Winona."

"Now I know why." Paris checked him out. "You're hot." She held out her hand. "Hi, I'm Paris Knight, and co-author of Clones. It's our new blog. You should, like, read it."

Matt put out his hand and slapped it, lightly, once, before cuffing it. "I will. Later. Bit busy right now."

"Jess tells me that you play in a band." She examined the hand Matt had just nudged. "Maybe I shouldn't wash this." She turned to Katy. "Hey, should we be, like, getting him to sign our arm or something?" She eyeballed Matt. "Are you famous?"

"I'm well known to the neighbours of the guy whose garage we practise in."

"What position do you play?" said Katy. She had fallen in beside Matt, very close to his arm.

"Ah, my 'position' is bass guitar," Matt said, keeping a straight face.

"You're cute enough to be the front man, especially with that hair. Long fringes on guys is so tots hot. Hey, Paris, we should take a selfie with him for Clones."

Paris nodded, emphatically. "Is Maddy going to go to hospital to get her stomach pumped?"

"I'm right in front of you so don't talk about me as if I'm not here." I pushed away from Matt and attempted to stand on my own. I did a pretty good job, too, until my big fat feet tripped me up. Matt hauled me back to the standing position where I swayed.

"I'm fine. See? I don't need saving after all. Run along now," I called, flapping my arms. The gesture soon turned into windmilling as I attempted to stay afloat. Matt caught me before I hit the ground.

He sighed, "I'm going to have to carry her," and lifted me right up. I put my arms around his neck and blew in his ear.

"Stop that."

Katy laughed. "What's she on?"

"Hard to say. But I doubt she'll remember any of this in the morning."

"We're staying with you. We don't want to miss a thing. Do we, Paris?"

Paris nodded and declared, "When my mum gets like this she goes all sloppy and cries a lot and then passes out till lunchtime."

"I had one drink, for god's sake." With my feet off the ground, I no longer felt as woozy, "Maybe two." I even managed to focus on my surroundings. The first thing I noticed was that Winona was standing very close to Matt. In the moonlight I could just make out his rock star stubble and the fact that they would make a gorgeous couple. Bile rose up into my throat.

"Put me down. I'm going to be sick," I said and Matt quickly tipped me off. I dry retched with my hands on my thighs and my skirt fluttering up behind and my hair swinging around my face until my head throbbed. I straightened up.

"No I'm not." I set off down the beach. The moon had dropped like a stone, making silver ripples in the ocean.

"Great, but let's go this way," said Winona, quickly catching up to me and twirling me to face towards home.

Matt held his phone up high with the torch switched on to form a wide arc in front of our feet. He kept sweeping it, lighthouse-style, over pieces of driftwood, an abandoned sandcastle with a moat, a lost sunhat. The younger girls trailed behind us, whispering about Tugwell's tiny todger, holding up flaccid pinkies and waggling them around in glee. "I wish we'd taken a dick pic and posted it on our blog. That'd be so funny," snorted Paris.

"Are they always like this?" Matt turned off his phone. We had reached the park's perimeter and I could stand properly by myself.

"Pretty much," Winona said, "Although, to be honest, they're not usually this quiet."

We had reached our caravan and Winona jammed her finger to her lips to shush Katy and Paris.

"Mrs Richardson will have a pink fit if we wake her or her children up; probably complain to Mrs Hitler in the office and have us turfed out." She clutched Matt's jacket at her throat as she bent down and withdrew the key to the caravan from underneath the besser block that helped to stabilise our van. "Which reminds me, I need to see her about my missing bracelet."

"What missing bracelet?"

"I lost my bracelet today. Or someone took it." She looked meaningfully behind her at Katy and Paris.

"It's not very secure," Matt said in a low voice, looking around, like he was half expecting the axe wielding madman from *Wolf Creek* to leap out at us. "Anybody could be watching."

"Yeah? Like who? The possums?" Winona said. She sounded bored and tired, now. She stood at the open door for a second, heaved a quick glance at Matt. "Thanks for bringing us home." She paused and added, "Do you want to come in?"

Matt, stared at her wan face for a moment, then switched to me. I tried to keep my eyes open, to hold his gaze, but I couldn't. After an uncertain second, he said, "Nah, I'd better check on Jess. She was fine before, but you never know."

"Ah, thanks for helping," I muttered, staring at the ground.

"You're welcome," Matt said.

"Are you coming inside or what?" Katy poked her head outside.

Later, in the dark, listening to Katy's adenoidal breathing, I sighed. I would not think about Matt

Armstrong. I would not imagine him catching a grenade for me. I needed to forget about him. He was into someone else, my sister to be more precise. I had to let him go. My eyes closed.

Chapter 12

At 4am I was suddenly awake, tasting grit in my mouth and really, really needing to pee. I listened to the sawing breaths of Katy and Paris, jammed my pillow around my ears and rolled over. Come on, back to sleep. I counted sheep, back from 100, found my happy place but nothing worked, damn it. After a few minutes of lying on a full bladder, I realised sleep wasn't going to happen at least until I'd peed.

The park was as silent and empty as a graveyard. On the way back from the toilet block, the laces of my undone sneakers snaking around my feet on the path, my mouth tasting like Velcro, I had that feeling, the same one I had at the barbecue, that I was being watched. But that was silly. Wasn't it? I pulled up short, peered myopically into the darkness, caught sight of the games room door, ajar, and sucked in my breath. Hey, wasn't it supposed to be locked at 10pm? I wondered why it wasn't. Maybe Mrs Hitler forgot and now a loved-up couple were inside on one of the leatherette couches, the broken spring squeaking like crazy. Well, I wouldn't interrupt them. I scooted past, but it was as hollow and empty as a cave. I remembered the bookcase in the alcove beside the fireplace. I could borrow a book – something by Jane Austen or the Brontes – to help me sleep. The light from a waxing moon flooded in through the fan light above the door made it easy to read the titles, *Da Vinci Code, Gone Girl, The Girl Who Smashed the Hornet's Nest*, the sort of thriller crap you'd expect to find in a caravan park, but nothing gothic. Not even *Twilight*, which would have done at a pinch. Then my attention was caught by a red and black spine. *The Gift of Fear*, its letters, black on red, making me tingle even though I'd never heard of it. But somehow it seemed to be asking me to pay attention. I picked it up. And felt like putting it straight down. Just reading the subheading freaked me out.

Survival Signals that Protect Us from Violence. I closed the book, thought seriously about putting it right back, but didn't, flicking the pages with a tongue dampened index finger. The chapter headings were a litany of bad vibes: *In the Presence of Danger,*

Survival Signals, Imperfect Strangers, Promises to Kill, Intimate Enemies. Holy crapola. What was all this? My heartbeat galloped away from me.

Crack. What was that? The sound of floorboards, probably, settling into their final hour of sleep before dawn. Either that, or the footfalls of an axe wielding homicidal maniac. Oh, yeah, definitely time to go. I shoved the book deep into the pouch of my hoodie, dried my palms down the side of my pyjamas and made like a banana split. You'd think, after all that heart palpitation, sleep would allude me.

Nope.

In the morning, my deep slumber was completely shattered by the horrible shrieks of Katy and Paris and comments, conducted right over my head, involving Alex Morrison and how he'd chewed up a twitching crab for a dare. Disgusting! I covered my ears with a pillow, but they went on and on and on …

It was as if everything from last night hadn't happened at all. Not the party, the joint, getting drunk, the bitten tongue or being nearly dropped on my head by Matt bloody Armstrong.

"You should have seen it, it was disgusting. Wake up Maddy." Katy pressed clammy fingers on either side of my face, "*Wake up*. You're getting paid to make us breakfast and we want pancakes."

"Go ask Winona," I mumbled through a squished mouth.

"Winona cook?" Katy sighed with great patience, "As if."

She shook me again. "Come on, get up," whining now and the next thing I knew I was being pushed into the kitchen, still in my rank old T-shirt that said *Keep Calm and Eat Chocolate.*

"Wait! At least let me shower and brush my teeth." There was practically fur on my tongue and I wanted to have a shower so badly I was prepared to have one in the morning along with the rest of the park.

"You can shower afterwards. Please," begged Katy. "We're hungry."

I moaned, but measured out milk into a Shake and Make Pancake container, replaced the lid and shook it up until my head rattled.

Slap, slap, slap. Someone was at the annexe door and I paused, mid-shake, my first thought being that it was Mrs Richardson telling us we had been too noisy coming home last night. I carefully set down the bowl and waited for the girls, who had also heard the knocking on the canvas flap, to go see who it was.

"Hi, Matt," I heard Paris say.

My stomach shot into my toes. Don't tell me Matt was going to see me in my pyjamas *again.* I pulled my T-shirt over my knees. Over my dead body. I inched like a crab towards the bedroom, squeezing through the gaping concertina door and, from low down, yanking it across behind me, the sound of it snapping shut, *snick*, like that of a clutch purse.

Winona lay, fast asleep, on her stomach. I scuttled forward.

"Pssst, wake up."

"Hmmmm." She didn't move.

"Winona. Wake up. Have you got something I can put on?"

"Huh?" She lifted her head, slowly, blinking at me with one eye.

"Matt's here and I look like this."

"Isn't that how you always look."

"No." I raised my arms out from my body to show her the extent of my wardrobe failure. "Open your eyes. Look harder, Winona. This is way worse than normal. I mean it."

Winona rubbed her eyes before feeling around for her leggings which she threw at my head.

You'd think that putting on leggings would be a straightforward task, but I still managed to get all tangled up. When I'd freed myself and slipped them on, I counted to three and stepped back into the kitchen.

"Hi, Matt," I said with a studied nonchalance that was completely undermined by a hair furball the size of a tiger's sticking out of the side of my head. "How's Jess this morning?"

"In a bit of trouble with my mum." Matt stared at the side of my head.

"Matt's going to stay for breakfast." Katy inched past him. "I've told him you don't usually ruin pancakes so he's pretty safe," beaming at him, "I'm kidding. Maddy's a really good cook," patting the seat beside her, "except she did burn last night's dinner."

"Because you were late," I interrupted.

"Sit down here," Katy carried on as if I hadn't spoken, "and tell us exactly what Maddy looked like when you found her. I bet she was hideous."

"I was not." I was excruciatingly aware that that's exactly what I looked like now, unwashed, my eyelids almost glued together. I made myself busy by turning on the cooktop and dropping a knob of butter into the pan.

Matt, on the other hand, looked as hot as ever, his coal black hair still damp and curling at his collar line, his strong arms folded, his head tilted towards Katy, nodding a little, as she gave him her most disarming smile that, to anyone who knew her, spelled trouble. It came in the form of 20 questions, fired like sharp arrows from her mouth.

"Favourite food?"

"Barbecue sauce."

"That's not a food."

"Um, roast chicken."

"Better. Favourite colour?"

"Black."

"Got a girlfriend?"

"No."

"Why not?"

"We broke up."

"Why?"

"She hooked up with my friend."

"Were you sad?"

"Not really, it was over anyway."

"Do you drive?"

"Got my L plates last month."

"Hobbies?"

"Music."

"Do you play any other instruments?"

"I learned the violin until I was 14."

"Why did you stop?"

"Switched to guitar and joined a band."

"What's the name of your band?"

"Thrasher."

"Why?"

"It was that or Vomit."

Standing at the stove, cooking the breakfast, I wondered if the name of his band came from one of Heathcliff's dogs. I smiled to myself, then froze, spatula mid-air as I tuned in to the next question.

"Do you like anyone?"

"Yes."

"Who?"

"None of your business."

"Do we know her?"

"Yes."

I saw from the corner of one eye the girls exchanging meaningful glances. I flipped a pancake, *Matt liked someone we knew.* Winona? It had to be. Then I remembered Sheila's advice: don't make assumptions.

"Do you want us to think of a better name for your band?" The questions from Katy kept coming.

"You can give it a shot."

"What about Kit Kat?" said Katy with a grin. Typical.

"That's okaaay," Paris looked slyly at Matt, "But IheartParis is better." She arranged her fingers into the shape of a heart in front of her chest.

"I'll run both those past the band. Thanks."

"What about Knightmare." I flicked Paris with the edge of the tea towel. She stuck out her tongue, good naturedly, then eyed the frying pan in my hand.

"When's breakfast?"

"Flipping now," I said. This was my specialty. I lifted the pan off the hotplate, gave it a good shake and jerked up hard, too hard. The bite-sized pancakes rose two feet in the air and then fell all over the place. Quickly, I scooped them up, hoping that Matt believed in the five second rule, gave them a cursory wipe down Winona's leggings before assembling them onto plates. I sprinkled them with enough raw sugar to buy our dentist the latest Mercedes Benz and turned, triumphantly, to present breakfast to the table. I was gratified to see the look of dazed amazement on Matt's face. At least I prayed it was amazement and not horror.

"I hope you're hungry," I said, shyly.

"Always."

What could have been a *moment* was spoiled by Katy's shriek.

"Winona! You're just in time for pancakes."

"Awesome. Totally starving," and Winona slid with her usual grace into the seat opposite. I shoved a heaped plate towards her.

"Hi again," she said to Matt, not bothering to look at him while she tucked her hair into her left hand and took the fork into her right. "Thanks again for last night. How's Jess?"

"She's grounded and sulking about it. But she'll probably talk Mum round which is not too hard these days." Unperturbed, Matt forked up another mouthful.

"Want a hot beverage?"

"I'd kill for a coffee," he said.

"Not sure if coffee is the word I'd use for these brown granules," I said, lifting up the jar.

"We could buy a coffee from the shop," suggested Winona.

"What with?" I sat down opposite her.

"The emergency money," Winona grinned. "Having to drink bad coffee is definitely an emergency."

I thought about the rolled-up sock in the bottom of my bag. Mum'd kill us if we used that for something as banal as coffee. Or chocolate which was what I was craving right now on account of the stress of entertaining the love of my life while resembling Garfield after a round in the dryer.

Katy paused mid-forkful, "What emergency money?"

"None of your business," I said.

"It is so," Katy wasn't giving up.

"We're not spending our emergency money. Anyway, I've hidden it," I said.

"Where?"

"Like I said, none of your business."

It was always best to shut down Katy quickly. It appeared to work. Katy lost interest, thank god, in the concept of emergency money. She picked up a deck of cards. "Found these earlier. Want to play some cards?"

"Like what?" Matt said.

"I don't know. Anything," said Katy.

"Strip poker," inserted Paris. Typical.

"No way." I not only didn't want Matt to see *me* without clothes, I didn't want him to see Winona naked. Winona resembled a Botticelli angel without her clothes.

Paris laughed. "Chicken."

I glared at her. "What? And you aren't?"

"Nope." Paris laughed again. I thought she probably wasn't, either.

"What about contract whist?" Matt said reaching for the cards. "That's pretty safe."

"What's that?"

"It's a bit like 500 but without bowers or the joker. It's easy. I'll teach you."

"Do we bet with anything?"

"No, we play for points."

"Bor-ring," said Paris but began picking up cards as Matt dealt them.

He explained the rules as he went.

"You have to say how many hands or tricks you'll win before we play each round."

Winona and I nodded to show we understood. Thanks to Gary, Winona and I were good at cards.

It seemed Matt was too, dealing with an expert wrist, talking in his slow drawl, our pen, with the chewed end, tucked behind his ear, keeping score on the back of Winona's history notes.

"We should get some music on. Get this party started," said Winona.

"I've got my playlist here." Matt pulled his phone from his pocket, and a little round aqua blue bauble that lit up when he switched it on.

"What's that?" My hand went out to cup the smooth underside.

"A speaker," said Matt, dropping it into my open palm.

Vance Joy's *Riptide* started playing.

It was fun.

Even Winona was enjoying herself. I could tell by the way she was sitting, with her knee up, and how she'd scooped back her hair into an untidy knot. She threw out a black three, I followed with a low trump, Matt, with a grin, played a high trump and won.

"Do you have some kind of card superpowers now?" I said as he gathered up his cards.

"What? Like x-ray vision or something?" He passed the cards to Winona to deal.

"Yeah, like Superman." I snuck a peek at him over my cards.

"Are you saying I'm Superman now?" examining his hand. "I thought you said I was Spiderman."

"Did I? I don't remember that."

"Yeah, you were calling him a superhero all night last night," Katy said. "It was embarrassing."

I felt heat rush to my cheeks. "I did not."

"I bid one," Winona said. "Yes, you did."

"You did," agreed Matt.

God. "Well that was pretty stupid. I mean, clearly you're not," I said. "Superman, I mean."

"How do you know? Have you seen us in the same room together?" Matt looked at the cards in his hand. "I bid two."

Katy and Paris kept falling into each other and smirking. I glared at them. "Would you sit still. Some of us are trying to concentrate."

"Are you going to schoolies after exams?" Matt asked Winona.

"Most of my friends are going to the Gold Coast."

"And you?"

She shook her head.

"Why not?"

"I was going out with Sinclair when we were booking our tickets and he didn't want me to go."

"How come?"

"He had trust issues."

"But you're not like that." I was offended on my sister's behalf. She shrugged.

"It was more the other guys, the toolies, that might hang around," she explained to Matt. "We're not going out anymore, as you'd imagine."

Matt didn't say anything. We played a few more rounds. Eventually, he said to Winona, "So, do you want to do something later? Like, maybe, go fishing?"

I wanted her to refuse. She had to study. It was my turn to deal. Act normal, I ordered myself.

"How many?" I said, shuffling.

"Two."

"Well, do you?"

"Do I what?"

"Want to go fishing?"

"Me?" I looked at him in surprise.

"Yes, you. Who else?"

I looked over to Winona, who hid behind her cards, giving nothing away. Katy pushed her way out of the banquet and went looking for something to eat. She found some CCs and opened the packet with her teeth.

"Maddy doesn't like fishing," she announced. She took a chip into her mouth, "She's a pacifist, hasn't she told you. I'm surprised. She's, like, told everyone else. Not very outdoorsy."

"Shut *up*, Katy," I said.

"Just saying." Katy offered the packet around.

Matt took a chip. "That's okay, she can take a book, sunbake, while I fish."

"Maddy doesn't sunbake, either." I wanted to murder her. Katy, oblivious, went on. "She thinks a drone will take pictures of her and put them up on the Russian internet or something."

Matt clearly wasn't expecting that. "Oh, right, I was thinking it was a cancer thing. But, hey, that's cool. We can swim off the point."

"She doesn't really swim in the sea," said Katy, helpfully. "Prefers the pool."

Hellooo, I felt like saying, I am in the room. It was time to take control of the situation. I smiled sweetly through gritted teeth at my two sisters. "Thanks, but I've got this."

"We don't have to go fishing," Matt said quickly, perhaps sensing the rising tension.

"No, no, I'd love to go fishing. *Love* to," I repeated loudly to Katy, who, with a swift glance to Paris, piped up, "So would we? We love fishing. Can we come with you? Please."

"No way," I hissed at them.

"Sure," said Matt. Katy looked triumphantly at me. I felt my mouth open slightly. This guy wasn't a superhero, he was a saint.

"Great," said Katy." C'mon Paris, let's get ready before Maddy changes his mind," and they disappeared into the annexe.

"Shall I wait then?" he said.

"I guess." I ran my fingers through my hair. "I really should have a shower though."

"I'll get the gear then and meet you back here."

As Matt passed through the annexe, I heard Katy say, "We can get a picnic together, if you get some soft drinks from the office and your playlist."

"Er, right," Matt said. "Will do."

"And tell Jess what we're doing. She might want to witness Maddy try to catch a fish."

It wasn't until I was naked in the shower that I realised I had an A grade follicular problem. I needed to take action. I walked briskly back to the caravan.

"Winona, I'm having a hair catastrophe," I announced.

"Your hair looks fine, just brush it."

"Not up here. Down *there*."

Winona came up closer have a better look. Her eyes widened, "You're telling me. You're a gorilla."

"But can you fix it?"

Was the Pope Catholic? Next thing I knew, I was staring at a tub of snot yellow goo that Winona had fished out from the nethers of her bag. Crap, what was that? It turned out to be hair removal wax. I was impressed.

"I can't believe you brought that with you on holidays," I said.

"For study breaks."

When the wax had been sufficiently warmed in the microwave, I sat on the edge of Winona's bed with my legs out.

"It's not going to hurt, is it?"

"God, yes. But it'll be worth it."

"What're all those?" I peered suspiciously into the tub. "They look like dead mosquitoes. Winona? Tell me they're not your pubic hairs."

Winona gave the tub shake, to check if the wax was ready. "I recycle wax. You should be happy. I'm practising sustainability."

"I'm not happy. Why would I be happy? They're your pubic hairs. I want to puke." I let out a bellow of pain as she ripped the wax off.

"Fricking, bloody hell." My eyes watered, and my skin started turning red where my hair and epidermis used to be.

"There. Done," she said, satisfied. "You can get up now."

"Thanks," I said, leaning back weakly. "I think I'll stay here." It felt like I'd just survived childbirth. Katy and Paris, as they crammed into the room, were my first visitors.

"Did that hurt?"

"It sounded like you were having your fingernails ripped out."

"That's what it felt like."

"Let me see." Two heads loomed towards me.

"Go away." I still felt weak.

"Let's go and find Matt. Make sure he's got everything." They took off.

"Thank god they've gone. They're like vultures." Winona went to the cupboard where she'd shoved her stuff. "What are you going to wear?" Her lower lip caught between two neat front teeth. "I've got that Tigerlily bikini. You can borrow it, if you like, and this dress." She held out her red button-three sundress. "This would work."

I shook my head. I didn't think I wanted to look cute.

"Why not? Don't you want to look good for Matt?"

"You make it sound like a date."

"What would you call it? Playing netball? Of course it's a date."

It wasn't much of a date if Paris and Katy were joining us, but I wouldn't complain. I took the bikini and dress from her and put them on.

"Nice. But you need to undo more buttons," said Winona scrutinising me.

"You sound like Paris," I said, undoing another button. "What if he decides I'm really boring? What if he runs screaming from the beach the moment I open my mouth?"

"Not this again," Winona said. "You're going to be fine. You're a Taylor."

Yeah, yeah.

Chapter 13

Maybe Winona was right. Maybe this was a date. It sure felt like it, I thought, as I waited outside the door of our caravan plucking at my dress, and when I finally glimpsed him striding across the park towards me, butterflies flew up from my stomach and practically choked me. He had the fishing gear strapped across his shoulder and a bucket hat on his head. Adorable.

"Hi," he said.

"Hi." We started off towards the beach.

"Hey." Katy and Paris tumbled along the smaller path towards us. "Wait for us."

They soon left us to run ahead. Out on the point, it was low tide. A nor-easterly rippled the green ocean and ruffled the feathers of circling gulls.

Matt set the bucket hat far back on his head and we silently picked our way around the rocks. I opened my mouth to say something clever *and* interesting – and failed miserably.

"Have you ever caught a shoe?"

We passed a couple the colour and texture of a leather belt. Nearby, a father chased after twin toddlers with chubby legs, calling out in a shrill voice, "I'm going to catch you and gobble you up," the kids squealing with delight, Katy and Paris, too, until we turned the point, a place where the green sea bled into deep turquoise. Matt offloaded the fishing basket and threw down his rod.

"This is the spot."

"We're going to sit over here." Katy made a show of spreading her towel about 50 metres away. "Give you some privacy."

I lifted my glasses onto my head to look around me. We were on a rock platform, pock marked from a million years of rain, with no one around us except for sea birds and sea spray. I looked back to the beach, the way we'd come. It was a tiny yellow ribbon winding around the coast that disappeared into a hazy horizon towards Sapphire Beach. I tiptoed to the edge and peered down. Waves shattered on the exposed ledge below and seethed across its sharp edges, draining away into an angry mass of swirling white and covering me in fine sea spray.

I was aware of Matt looking at me as I threw down my bag and wiped my face with the edge of my towel.

"What do you think?"

"It's awesome and amazing. Incredible." I ran out of superlatives.

"I knew you'd like it."

We laid out our towels, smoothing the corners with our feet and stepped back to survey our handiwork. They looked like twin beds shoved together in a motel room, or I thought so, which was embarrassing. I reached for the sunscreen.

"Let me," said Matt. He shifted around behind me and squirted the sunscreen into the palm of his hand. He lowered the straps of my dress, and rubbed along my shoulder blades with long strokes until my toes began to tingle. Just when I thought I wouldn't be able to take any more, he said, "Done," and put down the bottle. "Now all you have to worry about is the Russian space drone."

"Now do us," demanded Paris racing over to present her back.

"And mine," said Katy, pushing in.

Afterwards, she wriggled ecstatically and gave me moon eyes.

"We're going around there," Paris said, waggling a finger at a big duck-shaped rock to our south.

He pushed his hat back with a finger and squinted out at the wind whipping up the ocean. "Okay, but no further," he warned. "And no swimming. There's a rip."

"What are you going to do while we're gone?" said Katy slyly.

"Teach Maddy how to fish."

I looked doubtfully at him.

"It's easy. We'll start by baiting the hook." Matt opened up an old tin of half frozen grey prawns. I looked on in horror.

"You don't want me to touch those, do you?"

"You just have to thread the hook through his head. Like this, and then you cast off like this. See? Easy. Now you do it."

I reached for one tentatively, "They're slimy. And they stink."

"It's not that bad. You can do it."

"I really can't. I'm pretty sure I'm a Buddhist. I respect all living things."

"These prawns are already dead," Matt said. "What are you doing now?" I had crouched over a rockpool to plunge in my arms up to my elbows.

"Getting prawn slime off me," I said rubbing my arms. Matt shook his head, arms crossed, laughing eyes on me.

"Such a girl."

I squinted up at him. "What's that supposed to mean?"

"Nothing." He picked up his rod. "Let's just fish."

A seagull swooped down and stole the prawn I'd carefully laid down at my feet.

I clambered to my feet. "If you mean I have feelings and I shave my armpits, then yes, I am a girl. But I am also a feminist. I believe I have a right to the same things as guys."

Matt rocked back on his heels, palms up. "Easy does it. I'm on your side."

I folded my arms. "Doesn't look like it to me."

"Well I am. I totally agree with you. Women are definitely equal to men. Better, actually."

"Then why are women paid 17 percent less than men for the same work?"

"That's totally wrong, man. I mean, I didn't know that."

"Yeah, exactly." Some girls hated the word feminist or called themselves anti-feminist, but I didn't get that. Seriously, what girl doesn't want the vote and the right to an education and to work and to not be owned by her husband?

"You can see why I'm a feminist," I said. "But am I a bra burner? That's a good question. And I'd have to say I'm not. I mean at $50 a pop they are far too fricking expensive." I put my hands on my hips. "I'm practical. I'm a practising practical feminist."

"Smart, I'd call it. And cute."

"What's that supposed to mean?" Once again I eyed him suspiciously.

"Nothing. Just means I like you."

"Well, that's all right then." I tossed my hair back in that alluring way models were paid for in hair commercials but got my fingers snagged in a knot.

"Will we fish now?" Matt said, pretending not to notice.

"Sure," I said, though I would rather have napped. Arguing always made me feel wrung out and exhausted. *So* exhausted.

"Actually, I'll just have a little rest first," and I subsided onto my towel.

Lying there I wondered what Mum would have made of my feminist stance. She was always on about the fight but, sometimes, she made me feel that reading romance novels and baking were not hobbies a modern woman should pursue; that I should be signing up for pure maths and rocket science. I couldn't help it that I liked food technology and putting things in Tupperware. Besides, didn't feminism mean not just political, financial and professional equality but being allowed to make a choice. I tried to call myself a humanist for a while; someone who believed in the rights of everyone. But I stopped. It sounded a bit like I went around the place naked.

What would Matt look like naked? I glanced over. Hot. Yikes. I almost whimpered.

"What's wrong now?" Matt was staring at me.

I covered my face with an arm. "I feel weird."

"Sunstroke weird or weird weird?"

"Confused weird."

"What are you confused about?"

"Nothing," I mumbled through a sweaty elbow.

Matt flopped down beside me. "Jess told me your mum works for the Equal Rights Commissioner, right?"

"Sometimes," I said. I rolled over and rested a chin in a palm.

"Is Winona a feminist, too?"

"Ha," I snorted through my nose. "Just you try calling her a feminist. See what happens to your gonads then, mister." I thought about my way-too-beautiful sister and how she looked when my mother tore up the model agent's card. "Mum doesn't want girls to be objectified, especially her own daughters. Winona reckons feminism is Mum's way of getting out of the house while she traps us inside it to study and clean like slaves."

"So, what's Sinclair like?" Matt said.

I stiffened. So, here I was thinking he liked me, not Winona and all the time Matt was trying to size up the competition.

"Well, if you want to know, he's perfect," I said.

"How do you mean?"

"Let's see," I put up my fingers as I made a list, "He's very good looking, smart, isn't afraid of spiders. He plays a lot of sport. He's very into Winona. I mean, last month he got this radio station to dedicate a song to her."

"Really?"

I nodded, looking up at the fluffy clouds and the birds, anywhere but at Matt. I felt uncomfortable talking about Winona and Sinclair with Matt.

"Will they get back together, do you think?"

I tugged at my lip. "I used to think they were made for each other, like white dresses and confetti."

"And now?"

"I'm not so sure."

Could I be imagining it? Or did Matt seem relieved about the fact that probably Winona and Sinclair weren't going to live happily ever after?

I became aware of droplets of water flicking across my back and Katy's voice, from above, calling my name. The girls had returned and stood over us, drippy drops all over my back from seaweed they'd collected.

"Paris and me are going back, okay?"

I squinted up at Katy. "Don't you want to fish?"

"Nah," Katy said. She jiggled impatiently from one bare foot to another.

"Huh, well, I guess." I raised my hand to my eyes to check out the distance we were from the caravan park entrance. "But make sure you go straight back."

Both girls nodded emphatically and with a sincerity that would have warned me, had I not been so preoccupied with Matt.

As the girls turned into squiggles along the beach, Matt and I switched to talking about other things.

"So, what's your school like? What subjects do you have?"

"Umm, let's see. It's your typical selective school, lots of, like" – I pulled an angsty face – "Argggg. Subject wise, I'm doing biology, chemistry, history, English, food tech, which is kinda like chemistry but with flour and water. Not maths. I hate maths. Or, rather, it hates me." I blew out my fringe. "What about you?"

"Similar except I don't hate maths. I'm also doing music."

"I suppose you're doing three unit maths or something freaky."

"Four, actually."

"Hey, wow. You and numbers are like this then," – I held up two crossed fingers – "I'm thinking about doing four units of English."

"No way!" Matt sounded impressed. "Does that come from your mum or your dad?"

"Dad, I think. He writes poetry and stuff. Mum is more into anthropology and social science."

"Is that what you want to do later?"

"No," I said, slowly. "Don't get me wrong. What she does is totally amazing. But actually more and more I think I want to create something with words,

I don't know, maybe write books or ads or plays or something."

"So, maybe a communications degree then?" He was close enough that I could see fine hairs on his arms and the tiny mole under his left eye. My stomach did that thing again, but perhaps I was hungry – it was way past lunchtime.

"Yeah, maybe. I mean the ATAR is pretty high."

"Yeah, I know, about 98. But you could do it, you're smart."

"Yeah, maybe, I hope so. I did pretty well in my half yearly exams but, you know, it's only year 11."

"Start as you mean to finish."

"Absolutely. What do you want to do when you leave school? Play in your band?"

"Nah. I want to make music videos. Good ones, not the pretentious crap you usually see."

What about Thrasher?"

"We're not that good. I'd be doing a community service by breaking up the band."

"Is the name of your band after Heathcliff's dog?"

"I'd like to say yes and impress you with my literary skill, but we're named after a violent action video game. The guys are not that smart or well-read. Umm, I'm not sure they even read."

"At least it's better than Vomit."

"Agreed."

"Who do you think should have won *The Voice*?"

"Definitely the guy; the way he wore a skivvy with absolutely no sense of irony was extraordinary and deserved a standing ovation."

"Who would you have as back up: Adele or Katy?"

"Neither. I'd go with the mating calls of whales."

"Interesting. Where would you rather work, KFC or McDonald's?"

"I'd rather clear the tables at the House of Blues."

"Huh? I was sure you were going to say KFC," and when he raised up an enquiring eyebrow, said, "The safari style polyester uniform seemed so you."

"Man-made fibres give me chafing."

"What's the House of Blues?"

"Haven't you heard of it? It's in Sydney. Off a laneway. Full of really cool blues musicians."

"How do you know this?"

"One day, these guys from the Ministry of Music visited the school. They were way cool. Talked about that place. So my dad took me there one time when we were in Sydney. Blew my mind." He looked sideways at me, "20 questions must run in the family."

I laughed. We were both silent, then, and it was peaceful, the kind between old friends. Should I say something about his dad dying? Now would be a good time.

"I'm sorry about your dad."

"What? Yeah, sure, it's been tough." He ran his hand through his hair. "It was sudden. Although, if I really think about it, not such a surprise. He worked too hard, always stressed. Never exercised." His voice was as taut as a rubber band.

"I can't imagine what you must be going through." I dared myself to take his hand. Unlike Jess, he didn't seem to mind. "You don't have to talk about it if you don't want to."

"I don't mind. Actually, it feels kinda good to talk about it." He gave a twisted sort of smile. "After it happened, I sorta lost it. I was so fucking mad, you know?"

I nodded, waiting.

"I got into fights, stayed out all night, really hammered myself. Couldn't stand it." He lowered his head.

"Jess went all … I don't know … quiet. She spent a lot of time with Mum. They were a tight unit. I felt like I was on the outside. Mum had gone to pieces, couldn't even get up some days. She hit the chardonnay pretty hard. I was no help. The opposite. But Jess lately – she's been different, started hanging out with the wrong people. And this *guy*, I don't know about him, he's been hanging around the house. Mum can't cope. That's why we're here, partly, even though the memories are killing her. This was Dad's favourite place."

Dimly, I became aware of tears on his face, the pounding of waves, the seagulls. I felt his muscles contract and flex as he lifted up his shoulders, the universal gesture for *whatever*.

"Sorry about that." He blew his nose on the edge of his towel.

"Don't be." I turned away to give him privacy while he scrubbed his face, got himself under control.

I shifted a little so the sun wasn't in my eyes. "I don't see my dad that much. Since the divorce. Not that it's any consolation. Not really. It's not like he's dead or anything." I took a deep breath. "He's gay."

"I know," Matt said calmly. "Jess told me ages ago."

"Were you surprised?"

"A bit, I guess. But it was none of my business."

I was glad that Matt wasn't super fine and okey-dokey with it the way other people did to show how P.C. they were.

"So you don't mind?"

"Why should I mind? I'm totally cool with it – are you?"

"Yeah, well, back when it all came out, I wasn't. It was horrible and weird and we felt like freaks. It was a bit like he wasn't just leaving the family unit he was rejecting womanhood. I don't really think that now, I guess I was just shocked. I'm fine with it now." And I was. After he'd moved into his minimalist apartment with Gary, he became a better, more involved father. It was like, once he was honest with us, he was free to love us more naturally.

"Is Gary your dad's new partner? What's he like?"

"Gary? He's great, actually. I really like him. I don't blame him or anything. It wasn't like it was his fault."

It was nobody's fault. Nobody was to blame and everyone suffered, including Dad and Gary, and especially Katy. One morning not long after he'd gone, I found Katy sitting on the closed lid of our mother's toilet, a picture torn from a *New Idea* she'd smuggled in, pressed to her cheek.

"What are you doing?" I said.

Katy waved the picture about, gulping thickly, her face shiny with snot and tears and ink.

"I miss Daddy."

I wet a flannel and smoothed it across her face.

"Then why are you hugging Harrison Ford?"

Katy hiccupped and lisped, "Because he's handsome."

Chapter 14

"Want to swim?" Matt's voice brought me back to the beach and surroundings. I wondered how long we'd been talking for. Even though it only felt like minutes, it must have been hours. The sun had crawled across the sky to an afternoon position and fluffy clouds crowded in. I could feel prickly pink heat on my shoulders, the beginnings of sunburn.

"I need to cool off." He stood up, a man on a mission, to remove his T-shirt and I had a flashback of the last time I went swimming off the point and how he had held me against his chest after rescuing me. I caught the grin on his face and knew he remembered, too.

"Don't say a word," I warned.

"What about ... mermaid?"

Still grinning, he held out his hand to haul me up. I grabbed it and immediately felt an electric jolt all the way up my arm and I stared at Matt, pretty dazed, wondering if he felt it too and seeing in his expression *something*.

But before I could figure out what that something was, I was upended by a hairy beast that was heading straight for me like a torpedo. I rebalanced, ducked down to put my hands across my legs and felt a warm and wet nuzzle, a slobbery hairy snout that snuffled me all over. I heard a voice from farther away, calling, "Barney. Barney, come back here."

It was Mal's voice and the slobber on my leg was Barney's.

I wiped it off, Barney snuffled around the bait and I heard Matt say, "Whooaa, boy, careful of the hooks."

Mal loped up, growling, "Get out of it, boy," sending Barney into a crouch, and to me: "Don't I know you? Yeah, you're the girl from last night, the pacifist."

He swung around to take in Matt. "G'day, mate. Great day for a fish, eh?" Mal showed the dirty gap in his teeth, a regular bloke out walking his dog.

"Are you here on holidays or a local?" Matt asked, politely.

"I'm a local. Sorta. Me dad has a property in the hinterland, ways back."

Mal, weedier than I remembered, peered into Matt's bucket, at the bait.

"Caught anything, have ya?" He winked at Matt as if to suggest he wasn't just talking about fish. Matt ignored the double entendre.

"Had a go. They're not biting."

"Yeah? That's no good. I'm a hunter meself," he said, poking at the bait in the bucket. He straightened, hitched up his boardies. "Pigs, mostly."

I tried not to look at him – it wasn't too difficult. Barney shoved his nose against my thigh. He wanted me to throw a piece of wood so he could fetch it.

"Good boy." I patted him. Hard to believe that a man like that could own a dog like Barney. "How do you know, er, Maddy here?" said Matt. It was beginning to dawn on him that something wasn't adding up.

"Maddy and me met down on the beach and at that party, last night." Mal looked sideways at me. "We're old friends."

I turned my shoulder on him and said to Matt, "Hadn't we better get going?"

"Sure." Matt, though still quite not understanding the undercurrent, could sense something was up and began to gather up our towels and the fishing gear. Mal handed Matt the rod.

"Do you ever hunt other beasties, like?" Mal said, conversationally, watching Matt untangle his line.

"Umm, not really."

"Just wondering. I met this other guy before, sleeping on the beach, who knew a bit." He crossed his arms and in his sleeveless T-shirt I could see the edge of a tattoo, a boar skull in the midst of a dull blue and black rose garden. "Wouldn't have picked him for it, but. He looked like one of youse: from the city. PS4 got a lot to answer for, don't ya reckon?"

Matt loaded himself up.

"Nice meeting you, er, Mal. We gotta go."

"Yeah, me too." Mal peered at the sky. "Looks like a storm's brewing," one beachcomber to another. He scratched his belly, unperturbed by Matt's lack of response.

"By the way," still shooting the breeze, "I just saw your little sister and her buddy. Yeah, they were sitting at the bus stop." He threw the stick for Barney, "Good boy," as he slipped and slid to the edge of the rocky ledge.

"I don't believe it," I said.

He shrugged, smiling a little to himself, a private joke, as if it didn't matter one way or another what I thought.

"They were taking a trip in to town," he went on and his grin widened as he sensed me looking at him properly now. I could see a black hole where a bicuspid had once been. "Bullawalla, I'd say." Mal bent to scratch the top of Barney's head. "But I wouldn't worry if I were you. Those two look like they can take care of themselves."

"I'm not worried." That was a complete lie. I was worried, confused and angry. They were under strict instructions not to leave the caravan park. Mum would be furious, I knew, when I told her. But that wouldn't be until 7 tonight.

"Anyway, thanks for that. We've really got to go, haven't we, Matt." I wedged my sandy toes into thongs, hoisted up my bag and pulled my sunglasses down over my face to hide the fear in my eyes from Mal, who looked as if he was enjoying himself far too much.

"Bye, now," I said, keeping my head down, but waving like a mad socialite as I took off across the rocks, feeling Mal's eyes boring into the back of my neck, hoping Matt was right behind me.

We had hit the yellow ribbon of sand when Matt, loping alongside me, pivoted and aimed his fishing rod at Mal far behind. "What was that all about?"

"You tell me," I answered. Was he lying about seeing Katy and Paris at the bus stop?

"What a douche," echoed Matt. He waded into the sea until the water touched the bottom of his boardshorts.

I stopped. "What are you doing?"

"Emptying this. It reeks," and tipped the prawns into the sea.

While I waited, I gnawed at the edge of a nail. "I never thought I'd say this, but I'll be glad when Katy and Paris are standing in front of us. And if they have been to town without telling us, I for one will kill them myself."

"Let's go." Matt took off again. "I've got a bad feeling about this."

I did too. An image of a white van pulling up to the bus stop filled my head. I hastened the pace.

"Mal, or whatever his name is, probably made the whole thing up. Bet they're back at the caravan, sitting up there like Queen Latifa." Matt made it sound like a real possibility. So much so that when we arrived back at Paradise and I hauled open the caravan door, I fully expected to see them.

"Paris, Katy, Winona," I called out brightly, hopefully.

Nobody answered. I scanned the kitchen, Winona's bedroom. I even checked under the beds, nothing except for a strand of Paris's wiry dark hair on a pillowcase, a D.N.A. sample.

"This is so not funny," I said to Matt, who was putting down the fishing gear.

"I'm not laughing."

"What should we do?"

I stood in front of him twitching and pacing. "I've lost two sisters. What's the saying, one is a mistake, two is careless. Who said that?"

"Oscar Wilde. And he was talking about parents, not sisters."

"How do you know that?"

"Our school put on *The Importance of Being Earnest* and I was in the orchestra. Must have seen it, like, 200 times."

"Winona!" I interrupted. "I see Winona."

And there she was, Winona, glowing from her third shower of the day, hair damp down her back. I was struck by how calm she looked when I felt like there was a hurricane raging inside me.

I met her where the path bisected at the curve, across from the concrete toilet block.

"Katy's gone into town."

"No she hasn't." Winona was matter of fact. "She would have told me."

"No she wouldn't," I said flatly.

Winona's smile faded. "No, you're right. She wouldn't." She rubbed her hair.

"Well? What should we do? Winona? Answer me."

"I'm thinking …"

"We should call the police." Firm. A decision.

"That's a bit extreme, isn't it?"

"Okay, then we'll call Mum." I was eager to off-load this responsibility.

"Hang on." Winona raised up both hands. "How long since you actually saw them?"

"Don't know, an hour maybe. Or, maybe, two." I looked to Matt, "What do you think?"

"That sounds about right. Three-ish"

"And you've checked out the park? The beach? What about Jess? Has she seen them?"

"Okay, yeah, well, no." I began to feel a bit sheepish. "You're right, they're probably with her or in the games room or annoying Mrs Hitler or somewhere like that."

"Yeah, exactly," said Winona. "We wouldn't be so lucky for her to actually leave us in peace for very long."

Of course, Winona was right. I said more confidently, "Why would they want to go into town, anyway?"

Winona took a step towards our caravan. "Who told you that?"

I followed her inside the caravan. "That guy. The one with the hoodie I was telling you about before."

Winona disappeared into the bedroom. "Really?" I could tell by her tone that she didn't remember.

"He's a total creep," added Matt. "Talks about hunting and shooting and anti-social things like that."

"Seriously, if I can't find the girls, should I call Mum?"

"It's not as if she can actually do anything. She's three hours away. You're better off going to Mrs Hitler. She might have seen them or know something." Winona came out, wearing shorts and singlet top. "I'd help but I've got to study."

"Sure," I said, but a little part of me wanted her to drop everything and help. This felt like an emergency.

Emergency.

"Wait on. Mum left us *emergency* money. Maybe, I could use that."

I took the steps two at a time, put my hands into my bag and drew out the sock. It was empty. I felt sick all over again.

'They've got all our money. We have to find them before they spend it all."

Winona, seemingly unperturbed, puttered outside. Through the little oblong window I saw her drape the towel over the rope Mrs Richardson had put up between her caravan and ours. When she came back she said, "Have you tried calling them?"

"No! I mean, great idea," then, "But wait, bet I can't get a signal around here, it's like the Yorkshire moors in *Wuthering Heights*."

"The office phone, then."

I pulled a face. "And involve Mrs Hitler?"

"Fair point."

"Stan says you can get a patchy signal in certain spots and a strong one up that hill." Matt indicated to the far distance, behind the permanent caravans.

I turned to Winona. "Where's your phone? Mine's dead."

She held hers aloft and turned 360 degrees trying to get a signal.

"Anything?"

She shook her head.

"We'll go outside. Try over there."

Outside, I pointed towards the grassy tent area where it was less obstructed by gums and shadows. Winona waded through the walls and walls of flapping nylon. More nothing.

"You won't get a signal," a shirtless neighbour, his gut hanging out over a pair of Speedos, and relaxing in a blow-up lounge chair, said. "My kids have been trying all day."

I squinted at the tree-lined knoll in the distance. Sheila had once mentioned placing sports bets online on pension day up there because the signal was stronger and I started to walk towards the back of the caravan park where the grass turned into patchy scrub. Winona and Matt followed, Winona's Nike slides going whack, whack on the path behind me.

Winona pressed redial. "I'm getting something," and Matt and I pressed our heads close to hers. I could faintly detect the grassy scent of her fragrance. We heard Katy's high pitched slightly adenoidal voice telling us to leave a message, but only if it was interesting.

Little brat. I'll give her interesting.

Winona left a message, hung up and began to call another number.

"Good, you're calling Mum." I was both relieved and apprehensive. "Nope," and Winona stepped away. I stayed close. "Do you mind?"

She headed further up the hill, me still following. "I'd like some privacy."

Privacy?

"Who are you calling then?" I called out. "The police?"

"No, I am not calling the police," phone now up to her ear.

"Then who?" I mean, we were in crisis here and Winona was making social calls. I covertly watched Winona as she talked, her face all animated and beautiful. Who was she talking to?

"What are you doing?" Matt grabbed my hand.

I gave him an incredulous look. "To listen, of course".

"That's nosy and rude."

"I'm her sister. I'm allowed to be nosy and rude," I said, huffily.

"No, you're not." He dragged me down the hill about 50 metres to a grove of spiky banksia trees. I fumed, until I realised that once again we were standing very close together. Under my breath, I found myself making the noises you make when eating condensed milk from the can. I stopped immediately. I resorted to chat.

"Sinclair was in the army reserves, he told me once."

"Well, great," Matt said mildly.

I nibbled on my lip. "Do you think we should call the police?"

"Maybe. They'd be more help than Winona's ex-boyfriend."

I thought he sounded jealous. But then I heard a scuffling noise. Someone was on the other side of the shrub. Katy and Paris, I hoped.

Chapter 15

I pushed past Matt towards them, my mind already thinking up different ways to punish the crap out of them. Then my nostrils began to tickle. Pipe smoke. Sheila.

I followed the brown smoke to find her, dressed in an after-five kaftan with printed pink flamingos the size of dinner plates and hot pink sequins at the neck and sleeves. Matt's eyes widened at the sight of such flamboyance.

"What are you doing up here?" I realised that, in anticipation of it being Katy and Paris, I was using my shouty voice and lowered it so the "up here" part came out softer.

"Hello, pet. I'm doing my TattsLotto numbers. No need to tell me why you're up here." She cast her eyes elaborately at Matt, which I ignored.

"We can't find Katy and Paris. Have you seen them?"

"Not since they came past this morning looking for more brownies." Sheila eyed up Matt. "Hello," she said. "Your aura is very purple for a young man."

"It is? Is an aura, like, a disease?"

She squinted more closely, "You're the boy who helped bury Georgie Boy, may he rest in peace."

"That's me," Matt said. "How is he? Stan?"

Sheila shook her head. "Not good. What a terrible thing, and not the last of it." She tapped the rim of her pipe against a tree trunk.

"A lot of strange things have been happening around here," she continued.

"Like what?" Matt asked.

"Clothes getting nicked off the line, some food, such like. Yesterday, a bottle of my best sherry went walkabout, and I reckon somebody's been dossing down in the laundry. I've seen little piles of empty tins, mostly baked beans so you can imagine the state of the toilets."

I could.

"I tell you, us residents have had enough. We've got our personal safety to think of. I'm going to read the cards. Find out who it is. I'll have his nuts, I will." She gave her pipe another tap. "Now tell me about those two young girls. Very yellow auras, the pair of them."

"Hey, Sheila, do you think your tarot cards could help us find Katy and Paris? Except we don't have any money … Katy took it."

"Come down to my place, pet, and I'll do it for free."

And, a few minutes later, wearing the same tea towel on her head, "I see them girls. They are in a confined space."

"What sort of confined space? The boot of a car confined?" I squeaked.

"No, I can see drinks and sachets and napkins on a table and a neon sign above their heads."

I relaxed a bit: "Oh, like a café?" That made more sense.

"Perhaps," Sheila said solemnly. I waited for more. Sheila remained silent. I drummed my fingers, "That's it? You can't see an address or anything?"

"I'm a tarot card reader not the White Pages."

"What's in town?" Matt kept his face impressively straight.

"A couple of Chinese restaurants, a shopping arcade and one of those internet café places," she said, gathering up the cards to redistribute them.

Internet. Of course. Ever since they'd got here, Katy and Paris had been griping about their lack of access. I called out to Winona, who had arrived having finished up her phone call.

"I know exactly where they are. What's the thing that Katy loves the most?" I answered my own question.

"Her Instagram. So, where are they? An internet café in town. Sheila knows where it is. She saw it all in the cards. Isn't that amazing." I became aware of the tautness of Winona's face and ceased.

"What's up? You look strange. Who was that on the phone?"

"Liam. Apparently, Sinclair missed training. He thought he might be on his way here."

"Is that, like, good or bad?" I searched Winona's face for clues. I mean, it was bad for Winona if she didn't want to see him. It was also bad because Mum had practically banned him from coming down here and distracting Winona from her studies. Still, a piece of me was pleased. Sinclair was a capable guy; he'd be good in a crisis. Not that Matt wasn't, I said to myself hastily. But Sinclair had a licence and could pick up the girls.

Winona rested the back of her head against the caravan and closed her eyes. She looked rather pale. Sinclair coming down was definitely *not* good.

"It's bad," I confirmed out loud.

"There are some issues …"

Issues? What kinds of issues? But Winona, with her eyes closed, couldn't or wouldn't say.

I turned to Sheila. "What should we do?"

"Best thing to do is catch the bus into town, pet. And those girls will come home none the worse for their little adventure."

"Okay, so we'll all go, right?"

"I should stay," said Winona. "In case they turn up here."

I knew she really meant Sinclair. "Are you sure?"

"Positive. It's fine."

I squeezed her shoulder and turned to Matt. "You don't have to come, either. I mean, they're not your responsibility."

"I'm coming."

"There's a bus leaving in about 20 minutes." Sheila had been busy with a dog-eared paper timetable. "The bus stop is just outside the entrance, but on the other side of the road. That'll drop you right outside the library on the main street. Just have to walk down towards the BP service station, you'll pass the video shop, the IGA and the café run by that bossy britches. But you have to find the girls in time to be on the 6.35 bus home. It's the last one for the day."

She laid the pamphlet down and patted Winona's knee. "You look peaky, pet. How about a cuppa?"

"I think I'm going to head back to the caravan for a while. I've got a headache."

Matt went home to collect his wallet and tell his mum where he was going, and Winona and I went back to our caravan, Winona to lie down, me to spray myself all over with deodorant. Stressing out about missing siblings was stinky business.

The fusty vinyl warmth of the caravan began to close in on me. I opened the rectangle window behind my head. The breakfast things were still in their untidy pile – ants were marching backwards and forwards with the spoils – and Winona's book lay where she left it, face down, the spine stretched out so that pages were loosening right up. My hoodie still dangled over the edge of the seat. What a mess.

I was suddenly weary. My eyes travelled down the lines of the red dress half unbuttoned and sticking to the back of my legs, to my dusty sneakers. Not the freshest outfit, but it would have to do because Matt was there, in the doorway. He'd changed into black jeans, Foo Fighters T-shirt and aviators.

"Ready?"

"Yep." I jumped up and clattered towards the stairs. Halfway down them, I stopped, turned.

"Good luck," I said.

"Same to you."

We did the Taylor shake.

"I hope Winona's okay," I said once we'd reached the bus stop.

"Why wouldn't she be?"

True enough. It was Katy and Paris I needed to focus on.

Since there wasn't a seat under the yellow bus stop sign, we shuffled into the patchy shade of a gum tree. There was no sign of any other passengers or a bus, just a dusty car with Queensland plates coasting past and a half-eaten chocolate chip muffin lying in the dirt.

I crouched down to tie up my shoelaces, getting dust on my fingers which I wiped along the sides of my dress. My neck still hurt and I burrowed my fingers underneath the knot at the back to massage it.

"Did you ask Jess if she'd seen them?"

"She said that they'd talked about a place, the Beaten Track. It's got wi-fi. So you were right."

"Bet they're halfway through our emergency money by now." I remembered I didn't have money for the fare.

Matt patted his back pocket. "Got it covered."

The bus arrived, Matt used his Opal card for him and cash for me, and we moved up the bus to the back seat, past two pensioners in polyester tracksuits. They sat in the disability seats just behind the driver, with striped plastic bags on their laps.

"Are they both girls? I only ask because the one with the long hair is very tall for a girl," I heard one say to the other.

The other shook a blue-rinsed head. "You can never tell these days."

I hoped Matt hadn't heard. I slid in first. He sat down beside me, leaving about a foot of room between us.

There were not many cars on the road. I stared at the gum trees and asphalt making smeary grey stripes on my peripheral vision until I began to feel queasy. I grasped the metal bar in front of me. Matt looking over at me, said, "You look kinda pale. Puking kind of pale."

"I sometimes get car sick," I said, swallowing hard. "And bus sick." I put my head between my knees. "But only when I sit up the back."

He stood up. "Come on then. We've got to move you to the front," and, holding onto the pole with one arm, used his other to wave me out of my seat.

"Sorry," I murmured as I squeezed in behind the pensioners.

"It's not Ebola so don't worry about it," said Matt.

One of the pensioners half turned around: "Did he say Ebola?"

"Did he?"

"Ebola?"

"What?"

As the pensioners fiddled with their hearing aids, I wriggled uncomfortably in my seat. It seemed smaller than average and we had to sit much closer together, the edge of my dress touching his jeans. I tried hard to concentrate on the middle distance over the driver's left shoulder. I could faintly make out the radio station the bus driver was tuned in to, sounded like the golden hits of the '50s. I pulled a face.

"Feeling worse?" Matt looked concerned.

"It's the music. Dire."

"Isn't it?" said Matt. "I guess it would be too much to ask for Ed Sheeran to be played out here."

"Probably. Only got two kinds of music out here; country and western."

Matt laughed. We were silent for a moment or two, me trying to keep from vomiting, Matt looking out the window.

"So, do you think Sinclair is on his way down?" he asked, eventually.

"Who knows," I said. "He's pretty into her. At the taxi rank where they met, he said he knew straightaway she was the love of his life." I looked out the window. "She tried to give him the brush off. But then she hears that a lot. From the pizza deliverer, the lawn mower guy, my maths tutor, Barry the Breast."

"Barry the Breast? Seriously? That's a guy?"

"A guy from Dad's agency. He used to send her roses every day of the week after she did work experience." I gave a laugh. "Dad practically had a hernia when he found out. He fired Barry on the spot and had a long talk to Winona about what guys were like." Well, some guys. Somehow I didn't think Matt would be like that.

"Winona gives good brush off," I said. "A survival skill I haven't had to learn."

Matt gave me a funny look.

He said, "Winona seems, I don't know, more fragile."

"Interesting you should notice that," I said. "Most people think that because of the way she looks she is, I don't know, heartless or shallow or something. But she's not. Underneath it all she's a very kind and caring and generous person."

"I could tell from the party. She was really worried about you. Said you'd never been drunk before. Thought that maybe your drink had been spiked."

Spiked? There was no way I wanted to go there. I was about to insist I wasn't drunk, just tipsy, but then we passed a giant green sign between two incongruously swaying palm trees to say we'd reached the town of Bullawalla.

Chapter 16

The bus let us off in front of the library, just as Sheila said it would. With one final stare in our direction, the two pensioners took off at a totter for the RSL.

We stood for a minute, getting our bearings. Except for a dozy dog lying outside Leanne's Hair and Beauty, High Street was deserted, the air heavy with the smell of hay, brine and boredom. Next door, in the clothes boutique, a half-dressed mannequin and a sign, Closing Down Sale. A rack of question-able clothes hung limply in the afternoon sun. A beaten-up car cruised past, its radio, tuned to football, escaping from rolled down windows. I could hear girls skipping out in the carpark behind the RSL club, *my aunt plays the piano, twenty four hours a day, one, two, three …*

"That way." Matt pointed west along the main road, and we set off.

It didn't take long to locate the Beaten Track Café. It was wedged between a Brumby's and a Country Outfitters, for the tall and mightily proportioned. Was this a nod to the dietary habits of this small coastal town? A customer with a buzz cut and a burger and drink in both hands came out of the store. He stopped to shove in his final mouthful, chewing, slurping and rubbernecking us simultaneously.

"Do you get the feeling that we stand out around here?" Matt said, sticking his hands in his pockets and trying to look comfortable.

"You have long hair and I have all my own teeth. We stand out." I pointed to a hole in the council parking sign. "Do you think that's from a bullet?"

"Probably, but I'm too scared to check." Matt tucked a stray strand behind an ear and took off his aviators. "I'm not too popular with locals. There's something about me they find offensive." He stashed his glasses on the front of his T-shirt. "Here we go," and stepped through a curtain of flapping plastic strips into the café. I followed.

The place stank of trans fats and burnt coffee and was empty except for a couple of scrawny teenage mothers with nose studs and short denim skirts.

Katy and Paris were at the rear of the café, squashed in front of a giant picture of a Hawaiian beach, thumbs on phones and, thanks to our emergency money, well on the way to developing type-two diabetes judging from the remnants of milkshakes, hamburgers and ketchup stained fries. They were so intent on whatever was on the screen they didn't see us at first.

We loomed over them and I put two hands down on the table.

"You are in deep shit."

"Oh," said Katy, looking up. "It's you." She didn't sound very scared, or pleased, to see us.

"Yeah, it's me. And you're in the biggest trouble of all time running off like that with all our money," I gave her nose a firmish squeeze – oh all right, it was a pinch.

"Owww." Katy squirmed beneath me.

"And we want that money back."

Katy gave me an annoying little smile, and said through a blocked nose. "No can do. Spent it."

"All of it? You've got to be kidding me?" I looked in disbelief from one girl to the other. "We're going straight to the ATM and you're going to pay that back. Every. Single. Cent. Use your birthday money, your pocket money, your university fund, I don't care."

Katy struggled free. "Whatever," and turned back to her phone.

Paris swivelled her body around to partly obscure her screen and peered up at me myopically. "You should see my bank account. I've got loads."

"Then why didn't you use some of that?" I said through gritted teeth.

"I don't know. I guess because we had all that emergency money."

"Yeah, for an emergency. Not for this." I waved my arms around. "Let's go."

"Not keeping up our streaking is *so* an emergency," Paris said.

Katy, still swiping, said, "Look, can you just wait a few minutes? I want to finish up."

"No way. We're leaving right now."

Matt coughed politely. "Actually, it's still a 20-minute wait for the bus so technically we don't have to leave right now."

"Arrgg," Paris groaned. "Not the bus again. It practically broke down on the way here." She glanced across at Matt. "Don't you have a car?"

"Nope, sorry," said Matt cheerfully.

"What kind of boyfriend are you, then?" Paris then leaned her elbow on Katy's shoulder and lightly touched the screen. "Change that."

"Good idea." Katy's tongue touched her upper lip in concentration.

"What's that you're doing?" said Matt, peering at the screen.

"We're creating a new blog," said Paris. "Knight and Tay. Do you get it? Like Night and Day, the story of our lives 24/7."

Oh, good grief.

"What do you do that's so interesting it has to be recorded 24 hours a day?" I pulled at the nearest chair. It was stuck in the legs of the table and I made a lot of noise untangling it. The waitress saw me and darted out from behind the counter. "If you're staying, you'll have to order something."

"We're not staying." I pushed the chair back, grabbed at Katy's forearm and pulled. She shook me off.

"Hey, what do you think you're doing?"

Paris explained, "You heard Matt, we've still got 20 minutes left. Why don't you order something? The waitress here gets real grouchy if you try to use their wi-fi without ordering something more than water."

But I'd had enough. "I really, really don't care. We're going." I grabbed both girls by the arm and yanked them to their feet. "Right now."

"Owie, that really hurt." Katy rubbed her arm. "I'm calling the Department of Social Services."

"Then I'll call the police." A stupid thing to say, I know, but I was getting super mad.

"I knew you'd be like this. You're worse than Mum," said Katy. "That's why we didn't tell you in the first place."

She appealed to Matt, "Can't you get this lunatic to take a chill pill."

"Er, not really." He took his glasses off the yoke of his T-shirt and put them on. "She's right. Let's move it."

I held out my hand and after a furious beat, Katy pulled out three crumpled $20 bills, a $50 and some change, the last of the money, and slammed it into my hand. "There. Take it."

"Thank you." I smiled sweetly.

Katy gave me the death stare. "We hadn't even finished. I really hate you sometimes. I mean it."

"Get over it," I said. "We had to come all this way to get you."

We were on the street by now heading towards the bus stop. Katy, with one more stare, crossed over the road, saying, "I don't even want to walk on the same side as you."

"Oh yeah?" I yelled out. "How else would you two have gotten home. An Uber?"

"Uber! Why didn't we think of that before," Paris said, "Would have saved us from the sucky bus into town."

The bus arrived at that moment. Katy shouldered past me to get on.

"Come on, Paris," and they made straight for the back seat.

Matt gave his Opal card another workout and swung into the seat behind the driver. I pointed two fingers at Katy, then to my eyes and finally back to Katy to let her know I was watching her metaphorically even though she was sitting behind me. She ignored me, rooting around in her pocket for some gum, which she offered to Paris before taking one herself. After a few minutes of chewing, she made her way down the bus towards Matt and me at the front, sliding in behind us, breathing strawberry breath all over us.

"Want some gum?" It seemed Katy was feeling sorry for her behaviour. Well, good.

"I'm supposed to be looking after you," I said after taking a piece.

"Yeah, I'm sorry about that. It didn't seem like such a big deal at the time; I thought you'd be cool." She slid the packet back into her pocket with some difficulty. "What was I thinking?"

"Exactly. I don't think you understand how stupid it was to leave the park without telling us."

"Not that. That you'd be cool."

What kind of apology was that? I felt like slapping her all over again.

Unconcerned, Katy turned to Matt. "I've got a question for you."

"Shoot," said Matt.

"Do you like Maddy?"

I threw Katy my dirtiest look.

"I'm just asking because, you see, we all – Jess, Paris and me – thought at first that you liked Winona, well, who doesn't?, but then you went and punched Ben Forbes."

He did what? I swivelled to stare, open mouthed, at Matt, who, for the first time, had begun to look uncomfortable. Paris joined us.

"Yeah, Ben is walking around with a black eye and a fat lip," she said.

"For the record, I didn't touch Ben Forbes. I just talked to him. He fell over and did that to himself."

"Why did you do that, talk to Ben Forbes?" I kept my eyes on Matt's face.

Before he could speak, Paris jumped in. "He thought that Ben took advantage of you when you were drunk and high last night."

"I was *not* high." I looked sideways at him. "Really? Is this true?"

Matt waited for the whine of a passing truck to subside, "Well, yeah, it is a bit true. I did go looking for him this morning." He gripped the metal handle of the chair. "Get him to admit it and apologise to you for being a total dickhead. He swore no way did he do that, wasn't that sorta guy and so on. I told him I didn't believe him, thought he was a total prick and an arsehole and that you deserved better. And, okay, I shoved him a bit. But he kept saying nothing happened. I ended up believing him, but it was too late by then. He was all worked up and went for me. He swung a punch but missed and fell over and hit his face on the concrete. That's it. End of story."

"Or is it just the beginning?" Katy looked meaningfully first at Matt, then to me. Hang on. Matt thought that Ben and I had hooked up, that we'd slept together? I closed my eyes for a minute, wishing the ground would swallow me up.

"Why are you looking like that, Maddy?" said Paris. "You like Ben Forbes? Is that it?"

"I should have left you both in town," I hissed.

"Why didn't you?" said Katy. "We were absolutely fine. Weren't we, Paris? We could have got a lift home if we wanted to, not even taken the bus."

"You can't get lifts off strangers. It's in the kindergarten handbook," I said.

"I know that. Though he did offer."

He?

I spoke slowly, "Who offered?"

"That guy from the party. The one who tried to talk to you at the beginning of the night. Hey, I wonder if it was him who tried to get you drunk?"

Huh? I stared at Katy. "Mal, the wacko, offered you a lift?"

"Yeah, while we were at the bus stop. Didn't matter cos the bus came, anyway."

"Just as well," Paris interjected. "He was a bit rando, talking about guns with his dog breathing all over us." Paris pretended to hold her nose. "Dog breath."

"Yep. But *he* was cute."

"Barney? Yeah, very cute."

"He said he'd take us pig shooting. We were, like, '*awesome*', weren't we?" Paris broke in, nodding.

"I asked if we could post pictures and blog about it and he said 'yes'," Katy said. "Won't our subscribers go cray for that."

"And he thought we were 14." Paris high fived Katy.

Matt and I stared at one another. Mal was unbelievable. Paris misinterpreted our looks as ones of disappointment at not being invited pig shooting.

"I'm sure you guys can come with us if you really want."

The afternoon sun ripped into my eyes, whiting everything out and making me feel dizzy. I felt the prickle of sweat down my back. I wished I could open a window. But the bus rattled on and there was the squeal of rubber tyres gripping the road.

"Listen to me." I spoke loudly and with, what I hoped, was reassuring authority. "We're going to have to tell Mrs Hitler about this guy. Yes, we do, and you're coming with me to explain exactly what happened."

"But nothing did happen," Katy complained.

I twisted around to look meaningfully into her sceptical hazel eyes, "But it might have."

"Maddy's right," said Matt. "We've got to tell somebody about him. And stay away from him. No rides, no pig shooting. Nothing. Got it?"

Katy tossed her pigtail, and I couldn't tell if it was because she didn't believe me or just didn't like being told what to do. Either way, she ignored us for the rest of the trip which, quite frankly, made the trip much more peaceful, and when the bus stopped outside Paradise Park, they both stalked off, leaving Matt and me alone.

"I'm calling Mum," I called out after their retreating backs. "Don't think they're remorseful in the slightest, little brats," I said shaking my head. "But hopefully they'll be scared enough to stay away from Mal if he bothers them again."

Which I seriously hoped he wouldn't. I didn't think my nerves could take another altercation with Mal. At least I only had one more night of babysitting to go. Tomorrow, Mum would be back. They'd then be her responsibility, thank god.

I dragged my eyes from the ramrod indignation of my sister's back to find I was staring up into Matt's intense brown eyes. He had been amazing today. I couldn't have done it without him.

"Umm," I shoved a strand of hair behind my ear, "Look, thanks for coming with me."

"You're welcome. It was fun. Well, sorta," which, considering the humiliation he'd suffered at the hands of the girls, made me want to wince and smile at the same time – would that be a swince? Then I remembered that he thought I'd had sex with Ben and I began to feel, I don't know, *offended*.

Silence fell into the space between us. Matt seemed to have something still to say. I shifted my weight from one leg to another, waiting and listening to the staccato bursts of late afternoon cicadas. A toddler ran past us along the path, weighed down by floaties and a rubber ring, heading for the toilet block.

I realised I needed to pee.

"I guess I should get going. Fill Winona in ... and Mum," and made to go.

"Er, Maddy?" Matt stopped me with an outstretched arm. "Umm, about today ..." He jammed his hands in the pockets of his jeans. "I just wanted to say that I'm sorry about Ben."

"Oh, okay, sure." I hadn't really been thinking about Ben, but Matt seemed relieved to have gotten it off his chest.

I began to move along, towards the toilets when, "I can't believe you like him." It came out in a rush, catching both Matt, who was flushed with emotion, and me by surprise. I stopped.

"I don't like Ben Forbes," I said, slowly.

"You don't?" Matt, surprised. "But I thought ... Katy just said ... Jess told me you did."

The wind flapped at my dress and tugged at my hair. I attempted to hold both down, conscious of the families all around us sprawled out half asleep on camp chairs in front of their nylon homes.

Jess had said that? After last night's debacle in the sand dunes I could see why she might have. And, for the first time since the dunes, it occurred to me as I walked from the toilets to our caravan that I might have done the wrong thing by Jess. She was the one who liked Ben Forbes. Not me.

Chapter 17

Though I'd been half expecting him, the sight of Sinclair sitting up larger than life in the middle of the banquette seat, his arms outstretched along the back, the sleeves of his button-down shirt – this time a blue check – rolled right up to reveal his sinewy forearms, still caught me by surprise, and I reeled back slightly.

"Well, hey." Sinclair showed me his $10,000 white teeth.

"Well, hey to you, too," I said, looking around. "Where's Winona?"

Someone – Sinclair, probably – had tidied up. Even the cards that had been scattered on the floor had been swept away.

"Gone to borrow milk from the office," he said.

This was weird. We had plenty of milk, but I didn't say anything. By now I'd gotten my breathing back to normal, enough to grab a drink from the tap.

"Want one?" I said, in a hostess manner pouring him a cup and setting it down in front of him. I slid in beside him. "What's with the three-day growth?"

He rubbed the palm of his hand across his cheek, saying lightly, "Like it?"

"Not really, but it's not up to me."

Sinclair gave another of his easy smiles. "Think your sister will?"

I didn't answer. "When did you get here?"

"Just now."

"Did Winona tell you?"

"Tell me what?" warily like I might be talking about something else.

"About Katy and Paris and this rando, who keeps harassing them."

"Harassing?" Sinclair made fists. "Not anymore he won't."

"Thanks, Sinclair." I meant it. He was pretty strong, I'd seen him dead lift 100 kilos.

He leaned forward. "What I really want to know is, how's Winona?" He glanced at the door to make sure we weren't going to be overheard. "I mean, what's her state of mind? The last time I saw her, man, she was messed up. Cause we broke up and now, if she wants to get back, she's going have to explain herself. I can't live without her, man. I love her. But she's got to …"

I waited. No point, explaining. There was nothing I could say, anyway. I probably knew even less than he did.

"I can wait. I know she loves me, man. You know it. I know it."

"Sure, Sinclair. You were the perfect couple."

"*Are* a perfect couple. We're getting back together. That's why I'm here."

I got up again, went to the sink and threw down a glass of water, and another, wondering if Sinclair was right. Part of me hoped he was.

"Anyway, it's good you're here," I said.

"It's good to be here," said Sinclair. His glittering gaze took in Winona's unmade bed. "Man, you've got a cosy set-up here. When does Carolyn get back?"

"Hmmm, tomorrow." Too late, I remembered that Mum hadn't wanted Sinclair here. "Anyway, this guy I was telling you about …"

"Who is he? What's he want?"

"I don't know," I said, "But he's a real creep, I'm telling you. He's got a gun."

"A gun?" There was a flicker of something in Sinclair's eyes. Good, I thought. At last he's taking me seriously.

Sinclair flexed his arms and grinned. "I've got guns of my own. Say hello to my AK47s. First sign of this guy and we beat the crap outa him. Like, bam. Take no prisoners."

"I hate to break it to you, but this isn't one of your video games. This is real life."

Just then Winona reappeared. She had put on a floral blue dress that fell just above her knees and gathered her hair up loosely into a messy knot. Her feet were still bare and her toenails shone like glossy orange tablets and Sinclair's hardness melted as if it had never been.

"Hey, babe," he said, holding out his arm to pull her to him. "Where's the milk?"

Winona stood pale and stiff within the circle of his arm, "Milk? Oh yeah, they're all out."

She didn't look at all pleased about Sinclair and I wondered if he could tell. I felt sorry for him. He'd come all this way to win her back, the love of his life, and she couldn't bear to even touch him.

I said, "You're not going to believe it. Mal tried to give the girls a lift into town. They didn't take him up on it, but still."

"Mal did that?" Winona's eyes widened. "God."

"Where's that book I was reading?" I said.

"What book?"

"You know that book I found in the games room. It's all about Mal. Well, not Mal, but men like Mal. There it is," I spotted it on the floor and reached for it.

"Wait. I'll show you," I began to flick through its pages. "Here," dangling it open in front of them.

I stuck my finger down on the open page, and read to them a section on trusting our instincts, and using fear to fight or take flight." It listed the signals someone likely to hurt you would give – standing too close, asking too many questions.

"Don't you see? It's Mal. Exactly."

"But what can we do about it?" said Winona. "Call the police? What would we say? There's a guy hanging around here, offering us lifts into town. He'll probably just say he was trying to be helpful. I mean guys do that sort of thing all the time."

"There's a statistic here, just got to find it." I flicked through its pages. "Yeah, here it is. Listen to this." I cleared my throat, and told them that in California, more than 650,000 guns are sold each year, and each week more than 1000 get shot.

"Just as well we're not in California, then," Winona said, dryly.

"Driving around with a loaded weapon must be illegal," I said, marking the page I read from with my finger and closing the book on it. "I think Winona's right, we should call the police, the cops."

"That's a bit extreme, don't you think?" Sinclair pulled a face.

"Okay, well there's this survival plan. I mean, you got to hear some of these stories; they'll freak you right out." I found the page and began reading about someone being watched, and how she wasn't his first victim.

"I think you should probably stop reading that book." Sinclair took the book from me and tossed it on the bookshelf behind his head. "We're in Paradise Caravan Park, not downtown LA. And, anyway, I'm here now." He hugged Winona close.

"You shouldn't have driven down here," Winona, all quiet and limp in his arms.

Sinclair seemed to wake up to the fact that Winona didn't look happy. "Don't do this, Winona."

"Do what?" and even as she spoke, Winona began to inch away. His eyes narrowed and the sinews in his arms rippled as he reached for her. "I love you."

"Don't," said Winona, keeping her distance. "You're making this too hard."

"I've missed you." Again he reached out. Again, she was just out of reach. His face darkened. "I just want us to get back together. Is that so bad?"

"It's not bad. It's just … pointless," Winona, so softly I didn't think that Sinclair could have heard it. But he had. His eyes took on a coldness and he let his arm drop so that it dangled by his side. I held my breath and didn't let it out until he relaxed his shoulders and picked up the salt and pepper shaker. It seemed to take him forever to speak and when he did, it was matter of fact. "Nobody's gonna love you like I do." He began to simulate a battle scene on the table with the condiments. "No one."

And maybe I imagined it but he seemed to emphasis the word *no one*.

I watched Sinclair, lounging back in his seat, playing idly with the plastic salt and pepper shakers, pretending to shoot them down, and I could tell that he not only believed theirs was a special love but made it sound like a promise. And for some reason it sent a shiver up and down my spine and I wished I was anywhere but there. I glanced across to see what Winona was going to say, do. But she was a statue and it felt a bit like Sinclair under pressure was someone I didn't fully understand.

Outside, life in Paradise continued. The sun set, children played. I could hear magpies warbling. And inside the airless caravan there was a deadly quiet; a hollow space that would soon be filled by Winona getting up and standing, hugging herself, by the fridge and telling Sinclair, in a flat toneless voice, that they were never going to get back together. When he kept shaking his head like he couldn't accept what he was hearing, she told him there was someone else.

And that someone else was Liam. Sinclair's best friend.

Sinclair looked like he'd been punched in the stomach.

Silence stretched, taut, like a wire fence. When he spoke, finally, the sharpness of his voice stung my ears and made Winona jump. Though I didn't quite understand, somehow, I knew things were going to go south.

"Liam?" he repeated in a low dangerous voice.

Winona shook her head from side to side, "I never wanted to hurt you."

"You never wanted to hurt me?" he repeated, his voice still even almost conversational, like he was discussing the weather. You'd think it would be better than being screamed at, but it was about as sinister as anything I'd ever heard in my life.

"How long has this been going on?" He didn't wait for an answer. "You're a match made in heaven, oh, yeah." His blowtorch blue eyes fixed on Winona. "You and Liam. My best friend."

He got up. "I'm outa here, outa this crappy place," and started for the door, stopped, turned slowly around, raised up his arm, two fingers out, aimed at her heart, boom.

"Sweetheart, you picked the wrong guy."

Then, casually, he strolled out.

Chapter 18

In the vacuum left behind, I went from feeling cold then hot and back to cold.

"What just happened?"

Winona, still by the fridge, spoke through chattering teeth. "I think we just broke up again."

"So, Sinclair's best mate?"

"Yep," she said. "I thought Sinclair took it well, don't you?"

At that we both started laughing. It was a delayed hysterical response, for sure, and if anyone saw us they'd think it was totally insane, but we laughed until we cried. When we finally stopped, I laid my head down on my arms, looking sideways at the curls of dust winding up towards the patchwork ceiling.

"Where do you think he went? Back to Sydney?"

"Probably. I don't care," and she sounded as if she meant it. I was reminded of the morning Dad left and Katy and I climbed up the jacaranda tree out front to watch him leave, Katy gulping dramatically and waving a tissue. Winona's response was to put another slice of raisin bread in the toaster.

Just then, voices could be heard coming back along the path.

"Reckon they'd squeal?"

"Squeal like pigs, you mean?"

"I think they're adorable," Katy's voice.

"No way. They're dirty and hairy," Paris's twang.

"Everybody thinks they're gross, but not me. Did you know they make great pets? Johnny Depp had one?"

"Wasn't it a bulldog?" I heard Jess say.

I sprang to the door. There they were, Katy and Paris, crowding the doorway, happily discussing pigs with Jess as if they hadn't a care in the world and they weren't prey in a psychopath's spotlight. Completely forgetting that I was mad at them, I hugged them.

"Get off me," said Katy, looking surprised and not too pleased at such sisterly affection. I didn't care. I didn't know if I was relieved that their entrance cleansed the broken atmosphere left by Sinclair or that Mal hadn't gotten his grubby hands on them.

I turned to Jess. "Hey," and hugged her tightly, too. "I thought you were grounded."

"What have we missed?" Katy ran to the bed – Winona's – and starfished on it. I waited for Winona to complain and get her off. But she didn't. She just moved to rest her back against the fridge. Katy, relishing her freedom, used a big toe to prise off each of her thongs. Jess kicked off her Keds and lowered herself onto the floor in the bedroom with her back against the bed.

Paris slid in to where I'd been sitting. "Guess what? There's going to be karaoke in the games room tonight. Katy and I are going to sing a duo, you can sing with us as well if you want, Jess. Come on, it'll be fun."

"Bit cheesy, don't you think?" Jess said. "But maybe." She crossed a leg over and waggled it. "I will if Maddy does."

"Maddy can't sing," said Katy.

"That's not true," I protested. "I can too sing, I just get a little stage fright, is all."

"Well, sing then," said Katy, and turned to Paris. "We should totally film it and put it on YouTube. It'll get so many hits."

"No way," I said through gritted teeth. I hated karaoke.

Katy, who didn't, kept talking, to Paris, to Jess, to herself. "Let's go and help set up. What are we going to wear? Do you think the Tugwells will sing? What will we sing? Adele? You're coming, right? Do I look fat in this? Let's have a look at what you've got."

I nearly cried with relief when they finally left to paw over Jess's wardrobe and beg Mrs Hitler to set up early so they could practise. At least, they would be safe and, finally, Winona and I could talk about Liam and Mal and Sinclair going over the deep end.

"How could I not know you liked Liam?" I said. "Why didn't you tell me?"

Winona sighed. "Can we not do this now?"

"What do you mean?" I stared at her. We were sisters, and I was hearing for the first time that she had left her boyfriend for his best friend; and he'd walked out on us, leaving us unprotected from a psycho at best, paedo at worst. I needed explanations. I needed to make survival plans.

"Nothing. It's just this migraine. I've got to lie down." Winona ran her hand along the shelf behind my head looking for her earbuds. "Can we talk later?"

"What about Mal. What about karaoke?" I said as she smoothed out her rumpled bed.

"What about it?" She saw the look on my face, "Oh, Maddy, I couldn't possibly face all that now. You'll have to go on your own."

She shook out her hair, twisted in her earbuds and lay down on the bed, her dress splayed out, her hair, too, looking, with her eyes closed, in the twilight for all the world like Ophelia.

"But I hate karaoke," I muttered.

"Well, then, don't go."

"But what if the girls do something crazy like go to the beach halfway through?"

"They won't." Winona's eyes were still closed. "They're more likely to commit the crime of hogging the stage."

I was torn. Stay with Winona? Keep an eye on the girls?

As if on cue, I heard, faintly through the air above the dying laugh of kookaburras, the karaoke machine cranking up in the games room and a thin childish voice over the top butchering *Girl on Fire*.

I would go. But I wouldn't sing. I threw on Winona's grey hoodie, ran a brush through my fringe, mascara through my lashes and retied my sneakers. I gave Winona two Panadol and made sure she had a drink of water beside her bed.

"Promise you won't unlock this door unless it's me," I said. "I won't be long," and waded through the flickering twilight past a swing set alive with limbs and waving hair that smelled of shampoo and to the games room.

Chapter 19

I arrived at door at the same time as a girl with gobstopper eyes.

"I hope I'm not too late," she said, shoving her way in.

A boy with a double cowlick was next to push past, delivering dead arms with great affection to anyone he could reach. I edged closer until I was just inside the door. A tennis ball clipped my ear as it sailed through the air, nearly taking out a trio of Katy Perry wannabes attacking *Roar*. They squealed and ducked, shocked by how quickly their fan base had turned and scurried from the machine. Karaoke was tough sport. I pressed my back into the rough brick wall near the entrance and out of the line of fire.

Katy and Paris were up next, and they'd outdone themselves in the make-up department: their hair askew, their youthful faces obscured by the heavy-handed results of a raid on Jess's mum's cosmetics bag. They approached the microphone with grim enjoyment to sing three One Direction hits straight, each one more loudly than the one before.

The moshpit, obviously not 1D fans, grew restless. Someone threw a wad of paper. "Ged off."

It was one of the Tugwell kids, the one with the taxicab ears. I flicked him on the back of the head.

His arms crossed defensively, he said, "What? They've been up there for ages. It's someone else's turn."

Someone booed. Katy gave the heckler a rude gesture, caught sight of me and waved. I waved back. She gestured for me to join her. I waggled my head: no way.

"My sister, Maddy, is up next," she said, loudly into the microphone. I pressed myself into the back wall but Katy marched off-stage and straight for me, grabbing me by the arm before I knew it.

"What do you think you're doing?" I yanked back.

"Getting you up to sing." Katy braced herself against me and leaned away still holding on to my arm. "Come on, Maddy," she hissed. "Face your fears."

"No way," I leveraged myself away from her with a foot on her leg, tugging my arm at the same time. And that would have been that because I was much stronger than Katy, except for the pressure on my back of many damp hands pushing me forward towards the brick fireplace at the front.

"Hey," I said, twisting my head left and right to see who the pushers were. "Stop that. What do you think you're doing?"

I was propelled onward to where the microphone lay curled up in front of the dusty fireplace.

The clapping grew louder. Sing sing *sing*.

I glared at the crowd; at the eager shiny faces, their mouths split open to reveal braces and plates, globs of chewing gum and the occasional hole where front teeth used to be, their chant of *sing sing sing* more annoying than their chattering which soon became a roar in my ears. I could barely hear the music – *Titanium*, but I couldn't be sure – over the top of it. I started to walk off, but Katy stopped me. I mouthed, you wait, and mimed strangulation. She just grinned and made a get-on-with-it signal. I shook my head. I was *not* going to sing. I couldn't even if I wanted to. My throat had seized up. But I had to give them something or Katy would never leave me alone. Grimly, I nixed *Titanium*. I hated that song, anyway. Then I twiddled the dial until I found what I was looking for, snatched up the microphone. I looked out at my audience, grimaced – I would get this over with in as short a time as possible – opened up and began to recite the words to *Wild Rose* by Nick Cave and the Bad Seeds like it was poetry.

Beneath me, the audience gaped like they'd never heard poetry before and they probably hadn't. For the final lines, I lowered my voice to a whisper, then stopped. Silence. The audience stood there like statues. More silence. Nobody knew what to do. A single person began to clap. I shielded my eyes to look out over salt-crusted heads and sunburned necks. And there was Matt, leaning at the back, his hands working slowly, deliberately.

That got everybody going. They cheered, whistled, stamped and, as I jumped down and moved through them, towards Matt, clapped me on the back until I found myself smiling and thinking, hey performing isn't so bad, after all. I saw Ben Forbes. He had a swollen lip and a dirty look for me. I shouldered past, saw Daniel. "That was fucking weird, Taylor," he said. "But I sorta liked it." And he nodded like he meant it. I kept going until I was face to face with Matt.

Chapter 20

"So, you're into Nick Cave?" Matt wore the same jeans and T-shirt as before, but he'd shaved, and in a hurry judging by the nick at his throat. My stomach did that swooping thing it always did when we got close. Right this minute he was so close I could feel his heat and smell toothpaste on his breath.

"Anything dark and depressing, I'm not fussy," I said.

"You are something else, Madison Taylor." Matt's eyes, nearly black, were fixed on me, still with that intent bemusement, and it was doing something crazy to my insides. There was just about a centimetre of white space and oxygen – and not much of that – between us.

The swirling crowd pushed at us. From far away as if through a tunnel I heard our names, and Jess loomed into my periphery. She wore a sheer saffron yellow blouse over a black bra and her cut offs and Keds. She had a beer in her hand and an inscrutable expression.

"There you are."

"Here we are," said Matt mildly.

Jess sipped her drink and regarded us through half-closed eyes, "It feels like I'm interrupting something here."

"Yeah, well." Matt said. He took in the beer in her hand. "Where did you get that?"

Jess had another sip, taking her time with it.

"Why? Want one?" she dangled it in front of us. I stared at her. Why was she being so nasty? It must have shown on my face because she said, "Sorry. Do you, like, want me to leave?" her eyes going from her brother to me. Her mascara had smudged a little and her nails were freshly painted a poison green. I barely recognised the girl who'd sung Kesha duets and woven friendship bracelets with me around the Paradise kidney-shaped pool.

Go away, Jess," Matt said, wearily.

She laughed and pulled again on her beer. "What if I said no, I'm having fun."

"How many bottles of fun have you had?" Matt asked.

"Chill or you'll have a heart attack." Jess was careful not to look at her brother. But I did, and saw an expression of pain come across his face. It quickly disappeared. He said, shrugging, "You're right. Do what you want."

"Oh, I will." Jess downed the last of her beer and handed the empty to Matt. She used her free palms to push me to one side, away from Matt.

"So, when did you and my brother hook up?" Jess spoke low with glittering eyes. "And don't tell me you haven't. Not looking like that at each other."

"What's up with you?" I said.

"Nothing." Jess turned away and let her black hair half cover her face. Could have fooled me, I thought, rubbing where she'd shoved me. Her arms looked too skinny to have hurt me like that. Still not looking at me, "You're a user, Maddy Taylor. First you use me to get to Ben Forbes and you knew I liked him. Then you used me to get to my brother. You didn't even tell me you liked him and I was supposed to be your best friend. And now you seem to want to spend more time with him than you do with me. Not that I care."

With that she flounced off across the room and began an animated conversation with a couple of sunburnt girls, laughing like a hyena to let me know that she had moved on; our friendship was at an end.

The stuffy room grew smaller. A boy made a karate chopping sound and leapt off the arm of the sofa into the space right in front of me. I jumped. Took a step back into a warm body.

"Watch it." It was Katy. Dimly, I remembered that she'd put me on the spot up there on stage.

"Thanks for that," I said, sarcastically.

She grinned. "You're welcome. You were actually pretty good." She nodded towards Jess, "What's with her? Did I see you fighting?"

"Yep."

Katy looked at me curiously. "What about?"

I just shrugged and left it at that. No point in telling Katy; it would only end up on YouTube or as ammunition sometime down the track. Besides, I didn't want to examine too closely Jess's accusations in case there was any truth in them. I squeezed my eyes shut for a moment. If I had used her to get close to Matt, I hadn't intended to. We had always had a lot of fun together. I thought we were friends. I hadn't realised that Jess felt the way she did. Her dad had died, that was true. Maybe that's what this was all about? Jess was lost in pain and grieving for her dad.

Katy banged me with her shoulder, bringing my focus back to her,

"Hey, want to sing back-up for Paris and me?"

"Not a chance," I said. "Go find Paris, we're out of here."

"No we're not," said Katy, her face puckering up in her stubborn way.

"Yes we are," I crossed my arms. She could be such a pain sometimes.

No, we're not." Here we go again. Calmly, patiently, I outlined the plan. How we were all going to bunker down for the night and wait for Mum. How she shouldn't panic, everything was going to be fine.

Panic? Was I joking? Katy threw back her head and laughed. "I thought last night was awesome, but tonight looks to be even better."

I blew out a sigh. Was I being too cautious? I glanced around the brown box of a room with its busted-up bookshelves, grimy kids and jumble of toys. What could go wrong in the games room?

"Okay, you can stay. In the games room only. But only for one more song. Got it?"

"Yeah, yeah, got it." Katy darted away. My chest felt tight. What were those mints my dad used to chew day and night for his indigestion? Quick-Eze? I needed one of those.

Matt wandered over to stand beside me, his hands in his pockets. "There goes our budding pop star. They grow up so fast, don't they?"

I rolled my eyes at his parody of the proud parent.

"If she doesn't come home after one more song, I'm grounding her."

"And no phone until further notice."

"Agreed."

We stood there together like that for a while in companionable silence. Charlie Tugwell began to belt out Eminem. I covered my ears and wished I hadn't given Katy and Paris more time.

"Sinclair was here. But he's gone," I said.

"Really? Where?"

"Back to Sydney, I think."

"Is Winona okay?"

"Yeah, she is, you know. Kinda relieved that it's over. It turns out she's with someone else." I slid a sideways glance at Matt and was relieved to find nothing more than idle curiosity on his face at the fact.

"Let's get some fresh air," he said, and led me by the hand towards the door at the back of the room. "Excuse me, coming through, excuse me, excuse me," me protesting that I couldn't just leave, Matt saying as we hit the fresh air, "We just did."

Outside, the mood soaked into the black evening. The far end of the park was drenched in the weak glow of the park lights but here this corner was tucked further away from lights and blissfully cool. I breathed in the heady mix of early freesias and metallic sea spray and gave my head a shake to unblock my ears.

Matt still had my hand in his. My arm went tingly hot and I dared not move a muscle in case I spooked him into dropping it. Don't let go don't let go don't let go.

He let go.

"We'll go sit over there," pointing to a shadowy table close to the entrance-way to the beach. It was the same table we'd sat at that first morning. Then I wore my pink butterfly pyjamas and my hair was a bird's nest. I rubbed my cheek with the heel of my hand. Was that only yesterday? It felt like years ago.

"It's near the door, that way we can still see everything."

"Okay, that should do it," I screamed over the ringing in my ears. "Sorry," I said in an attempt at a normal tone. "I'm probably overreacting. I just feel like I'd better stay close to those two."

"I get it." Matt led us over to it and lowered himself on the bench facing the waxy windbreak. After a moment's indecision – beside or opposite? – I slid into the bench opposite. The cotton fibres of my dress got caught in the rough seat and I had to tug them free. He stretched out his legs, licorice sticks in skinny black denims and boots – ridiculous footwear for the beach. I wriggled ten toes inside my sneakers, also poor footwear choice. Matt caught me looking at our shoes.

"What is it?"

"It's just our footwear choices for the beach."

"Why don't we take them off, feel the sand between our toes. Live a little."

"Okay," I said. "But only if you go first."

"Okay, but I don't think musos usually get around in bare feet."

"I think they do. At least on their yachts and privately owned islands."

"You're confusing musicians with rock stars."

"Gotta dress for the job you want, not the one you have," I said, although personally I thought that Matt's wardrobe selections – dark T-shirts featuring bands no one else has ever heard of, denim jackets, silver rings and thick brown belts – was plenty rock star.

"I don't want to be a rock star," Matt said. "Whatever gave you that idea?"

"Oh, sorry," I slapped my forehead. "I forgot you have cred and want to make real music, not pretend synthesised pop."

"Damn right," he said. "Sex, hugs and rock and roll."

"So, does that mean you're taking off your boots?"

"Yup," and he did, laying them side by side on the ground. I lifted up my right foot onto the bench to unlace my sneakers. When I'd finished I put them beside his and wriggled our feet through the gritty sand until I felt something move, a crab maybe, or a snake.

"Well, that's enough communing with nature for one night," I said, quickly lifting both feet off the ground and balancing on my backside. The tabletop seemed safer still so I climbed higher. I peered down, but couldn't see anything. I kept my feet up anyway.

"Wimp." Matt got up and came around to sit beside me on the table so that we were hip by hip facing the sea visible above the row of waxy shrubs.

I heard a loud pop. Sounded like fireworks starting up on the beach and I wondered if we'd be able to see them from here. Matt put his arm casually over my shoulder. We stayed like that, me tucked under his arm and his rough denim jacket, in the starlight, contemplating the horizon bleeding into heaven.

Dimly, in the background, I sensed kids meandering in and out of the games room. Faintly, I could hear Mrs Hitler shouting and hectoring, shaking keys and threatening to shut things down if this noise continued.

"Reckon there's life after death?" Matt said.

"Maybe. Do you?"

"Dunno. Before Dad died, I was never one to reflect unnecessarily. But now, I want to believe in something,"

"Like God?"

"Hmmm. Not sure about that. My mum's Catholic and as a kid I went to mass," he said. "and, yes, I was in the choir. Until my voice broke. When puberty hit, all hell broke loose."

I could just imagine. I said: "There's got to be *something* out there, running the show."

"An energy, maybe? For a while, after Dad died, I couldn't believe in anything, not God, nothing. But it didn't help. I just felt depressed all the time. I think we need to believe in something bigger than us. Something better."

"I guess you've got to 'cause of your dad."

"Yeah, I suppose."

"He could be part of the energy field around you. Kind of protection."

"Yeah, like Yoda and the Force. I've thought of that."

"Did you know that on the census form you can tick a box giving Jedi knight as your religion? Mum told me."

"Is your mum religious?"

"Nah, just a feminist," I said. "But I believe that there has to be something out there, controlling our fates. There has to be a reason for the stuff that happens. Otherwise, what would be the point?"

"Like auras and stuff." Matt waved his palm over his scruffier spikes of hair. "Can you see my aura right now?"

I peered up at him. "I can see something shiny, but it's probably your hair gel."

"I don't wear hair gel. Hair gel is for pretty boys."

"Then it must be your aura."

"Thank god it's still there." He took his arm from my shoulder to lean back on both palms and looked up at the sky. It was cloudy and only a few blinking stars were able to bust through. The sound of laughter wafted from the games room, a heavy set rumbled beneath us and the balmy air wrapped around our ankles.

I shivered in the cool moonlight. Matt put his arm around me again and after a while I dared myself to put my head against his shoulder. He shifted his arm so that it was lower and his hand rested on my ribcage. I felt some pressure and found myself turned slightly towards his chest. He used his other hand to tip up my chin so that we were eye to eye and our breath practically mingled and I felt rather than saw his mouth drop lower and lower until it reached mine. The kiss tasted warm, like toast, and I closed my eyes with a sense of sinking into something soft and hard at the same time.

His hand on my ribcage tightened and his other hand came up to join it from the other side. He moved me closer to him until the top half of our bodies met all the way up to our lips. He gave a kind of noise in his throat – or was that me? – and our kiss became harder and suddenly we weren't fooling around anymore. It was not soft or sweet, it was full-on and intense and leading us to somewhere else entirely. I realised that somehow my arms had snuck up around his neck. With a sound halfway between a sigh and a breath, I released him, embarrassed at how quickly I had let go of myself. Judging from the way he adjusted himself and got himself under control, not quite looking at me, he'd been just as caught up in the moment.

"That was unexpected." My voice had gone all quivery.

"Really?" Matt said. "I've been waiting to do that for a while." He pulled me to him. "Goddamn but I'm into you."

All of a sudden, I felt shy. "I thought you liked my sister."

"Katy's cute, but a bit young for me, don't you think?"

"Seriously, I thought it was Winona you probably had a thing for."

"Nope. I have a thing for you."

Chapter 21

I couldn't quite believe it. Matt Armstrong had a *thing* for me. Not Winona, but me. *Me.* What did having a thing even mean? Were we, like, going out? Like boyfriend and girlfriend. Should I ask? What was the etiquette here? I imagined what I'd say: hey, Matt, would you, like, catch a grenade for me? What would Winona do? Nothing, she'd just know. She always did. If it was Katy, she'd probably check his status on Facebook.

Above me, the sky leaned down with damp, sweet, *haunting* silence. Faintly, I became aware that it was time to get up. While I'd been falling for Matt, Katy and Paris had been running amok and Winona had been lying alone in the dark.

"We've been too long. We've got to go." I half-sat up.

"Oh, yeah, I forgot for a minute." Matt had the decency to look sheepish.

But when we shoved our way back into the games room neither Katy nor Paris were there. We stood inside the door and surveyed the dusty bookshelves on either side of the fireplace, at the dart board, the shabby old couch and pinball machine shoved into the far corner. A solitary Red Bull can lay pathetically in the middle of the slate floor. A few remaining kids were sprawled on the crusty old sofa. Their tired voices crawled up the brick walls and onto the low, pock-marked ceiling. None of them were Katy.

"Did they go back already?" I was confused. "What's the time?"

Matt pulled his phone from his jacket.

"10 o'clock."

"You're kidding? No way, it must be wrong."

"Nope. That's what it says." He gave me the phone to check. There it was. In black on white. Twenty-two hundred hours. We'd been outside for ages, much longer than I thought.

The sound of approaching footsteps spun us around, hopeful.

But it was only Mrs Hitler. She was carrying the chain of keys and wearing the expression of someone who has just put her hand in a bowlful of cold tinned spaghetti.

"What are you kids still doing here? I thought I told you all to go home. I've packed up the karaoke machine. There was some disgraceful behaviour tonight. You should all be ashamed of yourselves." She shooed the kids off the sofa and out of the room and, turning, proceeded to do the same to Matt and me. "I'm locking this door. Haven't you got places to go to?"

"Hi, um, I was wondering if my sister came and saw you tonight about a weird guy hanging around. He tried to give them a lift into town. Has red hair. A dog called Barney."

"They didn't talk to me about that. No one who's not registered at the office should be in this park except when visiting. It's strictly for residents only. Is this person a friend of yours? Next time you see him, tell him not to use the amenities or I'll get him moved on."

"He's not a friend," I hastily corrected. "But, um, thanks. Did you see where my little sister went? After karaoke, I mean? She has braces, the other one wears glasses, about this high." I touched my chin.

Mrs Hitler draped the keys around her neck and held up three bony fingers. "They begged me not to shut it down. But rules are rules," she sniffed. "Our permanent residents are entitled to peace after 10 pm." She glared at us suspiciously. "So, please be quiet as you make your way back to your caravans."

Matt stared at her retreating back. "She has exceptional PR skills that are wasted on this park facility."

I worried at my lip with my fingers. "What should we do now? Go back to my place, I guess. Hopefully, they'll be there." I turned down the path that led to our section of the park.

"We should go via the toilet block first, make sure they're not there." He spun me by the shoulders so that I was facing the path that led around the back of the park. "This way."

Thick black cloud had scuttled across the sky snuffing out the stars and the moon. Even though we put our feet in the yellow puddles of light from the path lights installed during Mrs Hitler's beautification program of 2011 we were slow and clumsy in the dark as we swung around the other side of the amenities block to check the toilets.

"Ouch." I stumbled over something hard and metallic. What was that? A nail? Whatever it was it rolled away into the garden bed. I held my hair back with my hands so I could peer into the spiky bushes, but couldn't see anything in the dark. I gave up and peered around at where we had fetched up. It was a small gravel car park tucked away on the south side of the shower block, one I hadn't been to before, but thought I'd seen from a distance that day Jess and I met Mal on the beach. There was a picnic table on a grassy area next to a dripping tap. Further away from the circle of lights, the stars shone even more brightly.

Matt slowed down when he saw them.

"Check out those stars," and he kissed me on the mouth. I kissed him back but pulled away, murmuring, "Katy. Don't forget."

He groaned but let go of me. The light we stood under wasn't lit up. It had a busted globe. Better tell Mrs Hitler in the morning. Then I noticed the truck. It was a banged-up ute, white and grubby with spotlights and a bumper sticker that read Bring Home the Bacon with a picture of a pig and two firearms crossed over the front of it fixed to the back window. I thought about the way Malcolm had appeared at the beach, already checking out his prey. *He drives the coolest truck, he hunts pigs and carries a gun.*

I nudged Matt, pulled him closer to whisper in his ear. "Do you think that's his truck?"

I started over, but Matt held me back. "What if he's inside with his gun?"

I hadn't thought of that. I skidded to a stop, the gravel spitting out from under my sneakers sounding like gunfire in the silence.

"I'll go," said Matt, and before I could argue he had circled around to come at it from the bush perimeter. I breathlessly watched him shine the light from his phone into the cabin from the driver's window and then try to peer under the tarp. He ducked back out of sight and returned to me.

"Well?" I whispered.

"It's unlocked. There's a lot of junk in there. Empty Maccas wrappers, old clothes. An iPhone. Could be stolen. Dunno, but I think he's been sleeping in the back."

"See the gun?"

"Nope. But there was an open box of ammo and bullets all over the front seat."

"That can't be good."

The strength leached out of my legs. I put my hand on Matt's arm to steady myself. He put away his phone with one hand and wrapped his other arm around my waist. There we stood on the gravel and dirt, listening to the distant waves break and, at heartbeat intervals, a night bird calling for a mate. What the hell should we do now?

"What's that? Over there?" Matt pointed to a lump on the ground about a metre from the truck's front passenger tyre. A possum? Too big. A wombat, then? We crept over, Matt's boots making a crunching noise, and stood over an inert furry shape. The moon had finally come out from behind the clouds and bathed us in cool, grey light. Nearby, between us and the wire fence that separated the park from the state forest, the tap slowly dripped into a tin bowl. There was a funny smell, too, not bad, exactly, but sort of pungent, like sweat and hot metal and blood mixed together. A butcher shop kind of smell.

Matt picked up a stick and poked at the shape. It stayed inert and I began to get a very bad feeling. The kind of bad feeling you get when you look at something that was once alive but was now dead. This dead thing was tied by a frayed rope to the truck. My stomach churned.

"It's Barney, isn't it?"

"It's Barney."

I knew without looking that he would never fetch sticks again. I held out a hand as if to pat it, but withdrew it quickly. I'd never touched anything dead before. I didn't want to start now. His tongue lolled out thick between bared teeth. Blood matted the fur around his red studded collar and seeped into the ground beneath his head. The sand beneath its paws was scratched like he'd scrabbled about frantically before he died. I collapsed sideways onto hands and knees to gag noisily into the bushes.

"What happened to him?" I said afterwards. But I knew that, too.

"I'm pretty sure he's been shot," said Matt. He'd turned pale himself.

"Why would he shoot Barney? He loved Barney."

"It's pretty sick." Matt helped me up and we moved away from the shallow grave beneath the bushes, gulping in fresh air in choking gasps. I wondered what he might do to a couple of innocent – okay not so innocent – girls. Even though I wasn't cold, my teeth had begun to chatter. I wiped my mouth with the back of my hand. I shouldn't have let the girls out of my sight. Not even for a second.

"We'd better get out of here, in case he comes back."

"Which way?"

Matt took in the state forest to our right, the path to the beach to the east. Behind us was our caravan. He pointed that way.

"Let's check there first."

"What if something's happened to them?" I moaned. "What if Mal got to them while we were ... you know?" I stumbled. "I'll never forgive myself."

Never never.

Chapter 22

Long before we got to the caravan, we collided with an urgent trio of adults, huddled at the western corner of the administration block. Stan, his varicose veins blue and ropy in shower shoes beneath an indecently short robe and Sheila, in a lurid pink dressing gown zipped up to her neck, were talking to Mrs Hitler, the keys still around her neck.

"Sheila!" I broke free from Matt and ran to her. "I've lost Katy and Paris." I began to cry.

"Thank heavens you're safe." Sheila enveloped me in her arms. Her nylon dressing gown smelled just like my Barbie doll's hair used to after it was left too long in the sun.

"Safe from what? Sheila, safe from what?" but she wasn't listening.

Her thick fingers worried the teeth of her zipper as she said to Mrs Hitler, "I tell you, he had a gun. I saw it with my own eyes. Stan tell her," but Sheila didn't wait. She went on, "A rifle of some sort. Wicked thing, but not as wicked as the black soul of the feller holding it."

Sheila's face was loose with fear. Stan patted her awkwardly. "Now, now, Sheila. He pointed it at you, I know, but he didn't fire it. That's a good sign."

"No it's not. I have a very bad feeling."

Mrs Hitler didn't have much patience for Sheila's feelings. She interrupted: "I've called the police. They're on their way. At least it's the middle of the night and most people," she glared at Matt and me, "aren't likely to be wandering about to become targets."

I began to feel faint. "That's too long." I felt Sheila begin to sag under my weight. "Sheila?" but Sheila had dissolved into ragged sobs.

"That's why we need to get back," seeing Sheila no longer able to speak alarmed me enormously. Stan made every effort to rein in his emotions. He was ex-navy and he had a duty to protect civilians from danger. He retied his robe and began to marshal us towards the office,

"We should get inside and wait for the police. That's the way. If you could just open up, please," to Mrs Hitler who took off her keys for the umpteenth time in a few hours. Stan pushed the door wide and began to herd us in, looking over his shoulder and still talking, "It was a double barrel shot gun. I know the weapon. They're used for hunting primarily, but accuracy depends on the shooter. I don't know what kind of shooter this clown is, but a slug from that piece could drop a pig from a distance. I mean, he doesn't look like he could handle a gun. He was a snotty kinda kid; the type to have only ever used one of them video consoles. A real fancy pants, you know what I mean? Wore one of them checkered shirts with the sleeves pushed up, thought he was hot stuff." Stan clicked his stubby fingers. "What's the name of that pretty boy singer? All the young girls love him. Justin something or other."

"Justin Bieber." I spoke absently because I had been thinking to myself that though Mal was many things, he couldn't be described as snotty.

Malcolm was scruffy and sly. He was crafty, uneducated and poor. He might have fancied himself a ladies' man, but he didn't wear fancy pants; he wore cargo shorts with lots of pockets that showed his bum crack. And he was definitely no Belieber.

But I knew someone who was. Someone wearing a shirt like the one Stan described. A sudden spasm shook my body and I felt cold all over. Oh, shit, oh, shit, oh, shit. I leaned up against the door frame to steady myself. *Oh, shit on toast.*

I stood there in the doorway to the office of Paradise Caravan Park, not believing it. I glanced at Matt, swung around to the others, saw confusion and disarray. Fat tears coursed down Sheila's face, her eyes were wide. She'd seen the future long before me.

Before I was cold, now I felt hot and feverish. The rough wall bit into my legs, my mind put together all the broken scenes into a picture that was almost incomprehensible. I rolled onto my shoulder. What had he said in the caravan earlier, you picked the wrong guy? My knees were like rubber bands and I hung onto the edge of the wall, dizzy.

And how right he was. It was Winona, I suddenly knew, I should be afraid for, not Katy. Mr Perfect wasn't back at all. Not by a long shot. And he wasn't getting over it, *her*. I had to warn Winona. Mr Perfect was gone, if he had ever been there at all.

I pushed off from the door jam and began to run. I could hear Matt calling out to me, to come back. But I couldn't wait. Not for one more second. I'd already wasted too much time and energy on the wrong guy. Because I knew as surely as I've ever known anything in my life that I had made a dreadful mistake. It wasn't Mal we needed to protect ourselves from. The man we had to be most afraid of was Sinclair Reed.

The Scrabble letters had returned. The distinctive News Gothic tiles followed me back to the caravan, running to catch up to me as I splashed once again through the yellow light, slap, slap, my sneaker laces undone and flicking up against my bare ankles. The tiles were forming words, what were they? I squinted in the dark to read them.

Go quietly.

So I took a few precious seconds to tie up my shoelaces and slow down the heartbeat that was making me pant too loudly in the dark. How could I have been so stupid?

Stranger-danger is what we'd been taught at school. Beware of stranger-danger. So, of course, it was the face of the man with the missing tooth who had slithered into our lives, offering the girls a ride and me a drink, who I'd been focused on. His potential evil and randomness had totally mesmerised me to the point where I couldn't begin to see that the person we needed to be most afraid of was right in front of our faces, and had been for a long time.

What had the book said, statistically the man most likely to kill a woman is the husband or boyfriend. I squeezed my eyes so tightly shut I saw stars – and an image of splotchy fingermarks around Winona's neck that I'd seen in the car.

The caravan reared up like a silver beast in the dark and stopped me dead in my tracks. Words formed up again in my vision, same little tiles with a different message.

Make a small target.

I dropped to my knees and began to crawl past the Richardsons' place. It was quiet. But it would be just after 10 when bedtime was after tea. Everyone would be sound asleep. I scrabbled around in the dirt between the caravans under the clothes line, looking for a stick or a stone, an invisibility cloak, anything for protection. A listless striped towel flicked me in the eye. I gasped and took a moment to recover, sitting back on my haunches. Above my head, the kitchen window, dimly lit and slightly open, let out Sinclair's fierce mutterings.

"Winona, you don't know how much you've betrayed me. The fucked thing is I still love you."

He didn't blame Liam. His best friend. Some best friend. Girls are the root of all evil, especially the pretty ones who shake their booty in front of everyone. They're the ones who should be stopped, they're the ones, and he'd be doing mankind, humankind, a fucking favour. It was all her fault.

On hands and knees, I crawled along the metal edge of the caravan, feeling my way with stiff fingers like a blind person, until I reached the annexe. The gap would be small but if I could flatten myself out, I might be able to get underneath. To do what, exactly, I didn't quite know, but a sense of hope welled up inside me even though the damp earth beneath me felt like a grave. I could hear blood pumping through my veins. Further off, a branch cracked and the sea churned.

And inside the caravan Sinclair paced and muttered about death and destruction and liars and girls who deserved whatever was coming to them.

I pictured the bedroom where he was pacing, with the unmade bed and clothes spilling out of the wardrobe. The other girls would be in the kitchen, I knew it as surely as I breathed. They'd be sitting at the fold-out Formica table crammed with the detritus of boring life: cups, an empty Cheerios box, a book, lying face down, old yoghurt container, a spoon. It was a snapshot dull, ordinary life. Except that it wasn't.

Outside, a mosquito buzzed in my ear. Time, so long suspended, started back up and with such force it overtook me. Something inside me begged me to move. So I did, commando style, slithering under the greasy canvas flap of the annexe. I found myself in the tight corner beside the door into the caravan. I peeked inside.

There they were, just as they had been in my mind; Katy and Paris, sitting bolt upright, frozen in time and space, at one end of the table. Jess – oh god – was at the other, for once in her life, without that sneer. Her nose ring winked at me though her eyes were fixed on a point beyond my vision. At Sinclair, probably, who was pacing in the bedroom having a one-way conversation with Winona.

Yes, there he was. I could see him in the reflection of the kitchen window, pacing up and down, his hair smooth, like he'd stood in front of a mirror and worked on it. But his face had fallen in on itself. Mal's shotgun rested in his arms, the barrel pointed not at Winona but at the floor. I had never seen such a weapon in real life before. The girls were right about how small, innocent it looked. But at least it wasn't pointing at her head. So, the dumb arse would shoot a hole through his foot. Big deal. That's if he could shoot the thing at all. No way *Call of Duty* could prepare anyone for real ammunition, the real deal. For a second I was hopeful.

Then he raised the gun, arms straight and fingers steady, and aimed it into the corner of the bedroom and my heart stuttered like I'd just hit freezing water.

I could hear whimpering. It was Winona I could hear, whimpering and begging. Winona, who had once knitted me a long, narrow, multi-coloured scarf because Janey Tan had one and I wanted one, too.

"Shut up." A snarl. A pause. More pacing. Up and down, up and down, the caravan rocked with every step until I felt queasy. He wasn't wearing shoes, the white T-shirt beneath his open checked shirt and jeans rumpled and grubby like he'd been sleeping rough. The projector whirred through my head. I saw Sheila's stolen sleeping bag. And bones, frail, featherlight in a gleaming grey pile in the moonlight. Sinclair had been in Paradise Caravan Park all along.

"Man, I loved you."

It took a second for my mind to catch up to the words. *Loved.* The past tense.

That had to be bad.

He stopped pacing and I went from seeing the whole picture to a close up of just Sinclair's thumb. I saw the dirt beneath his thumbnail as he fondled the hammer of the gun. I saw the wrinkles disappear as he pulled it back. That clicking noise again. Then my sister's whisper, sounding a million miles away, but coming from the corner of the bedroom, just out of sight.

"Sinclair, please ..."

Sinclair stepping back, getting the distance he needed.

"Nobody's gonna love you like me, baby."

And a loud popping sound as he fired and then smoke. A thud.

Paris got the second bullet. She made a long sigh as she floated to the floor, her glasses still on her face. Collateral damage, her injuries would be called later. Sinclair reloaded, metal clinked to the floor. Jess half stood, turned sideways and sort of fell off the seat, the vinyl made a whooshing noise as it re-inflated so that the third bullet smacked into the wall behind her. She fell down the stairs. Sinclair let her go, turning his head an inch to observe Katy scramble to get out of the line of fire, all elbows and knees, making for the door. His eyelids sort of fluttered and he said, "Fuck that," not aggressive or mean. But matter of fact, like, "You're not leaving," taking two steps forward, arms straight out, levelling the gun with both hands, easy, his face impassive, like he was the avatar in a video game.

The letters inside me grew bigger and bigger. *Go.* And then I was on my feet. I don't even remember pushing myself up, but there I was, levitating over Jess's crumpled body, up the stairs, across the kitchen through weird blue smoke that smelled of firecrackers, arms outstretched, flying over the top of Paris and all that blood and broken crockery towards Katy.

Boom.

Chapter 23

A hard punch. Sinclair shooting me felt like a hard punch or a shove. The numbness started off slow, a lick that spread out through my body in the sort of tingling sensation that usually comes from sitting cross legged for too long and all of a sudden I wasn't flying anymore.

I was falling, down, down. I lay there on the floor of the kitchen of our caravan where we'd spent our holidays for the past six Septembers, with everything smashed up around me, looking up at the sky, at all the millions of stars that weren't really there, waiting for Sinclair to finish what he started. I was tired, so tired. I yawned. My lips were very dry.

A flutter of movement, sensed rather than seen from the corner of my eye, but it wasn't Sinclair. He'd already gone into the cold, old night.

It was the twitch of a foot, bare and white with orange toenails, upside down. But no, I was looking at it upside down. I turned my head so that I could get an idea of rest of the bedroom. All I could see was the wardrobe door gaping wide and resting against the wall. It was covered in a fine red mist and something grey and lumpy that stained the clothes inside on hangers and the wall behind. I closed my eyes. This couldn't be real.

But it was. When I opened them again, everything looked exactly the same, the foot with the orange toenails still lying about a metre from my face. I lowered my chin onto my chest so I could examine my fingers like twigs on the ends of outstretched arms, but they didn't belong to me and I couldn't make them move. And I wanted so badly to touch my sister's foot, so beautiful lying there, so still like it was carved from alabaster or marble. I made my arm longer with the power of my mind until I could get my fingers around the foot. It was warm and slippery and wet with blood – oh, god, oh god, oh god, oh god. Gasping, I lost my grip.

"Winona?" I said, hoarsely, to the upside-down foot. "Wriggle your toes if you can hear me?"

The air, still reeking of fireworks, was stifling. I reached out again with the tip of a shaky finger, felt the delicate bone of her ankle, so still. Please move. Please be okay. But she wasn't okay. Shadows gathered like dust in the tight corners of the caravan. I closed my eyes so I couldn't see them take my sister away.

* * *

When I came to, I was on the damp ground outside and a guy with no shirt on was trying to smother me … Something very bad had just happened, but I couldn't remember what it was and pressure on my chest was making it difficult to breathe.

"Don't move." The guy loomed over me again with the rock, but not a rock, a wadded up T-shirt, his. I saw who it was. Matt.

I wanted to ask him something, but I couldn't quite recall what it was. He went back to pressing down on me. Something really, really bad had happened. I couldn't remember what. I only knew it was something to do with Katy. I tried to speak, but the words didn't come out.

Matt pressing down on my wound made it difficult to concentrate.

"Did someone call an ambulance?" The question came from above me and to the side. It sounded like Mrs Hitler, but I wasn't sure. Another voice shouted, "You'd better call their mother."

Then an authoritative voice told everyone to get back, back up.

"We need room."

I turned my head sideways slightly. I could see a figure on the hard ground a few metres away. A guy in a short terry towelling dress was leaning across it, fingers pinching a chin and breathing air into a silent mouth. Stan. Who was he leaning over? Katy? Paris, her glasses gone, and I remembered: Sinclair had shot her, too. My teeth began to chatter.

"Matt," I whispered. "My hands are cold."

"No, don't move. I'll warm them up in a sec."

Now my arm was going to sleep. Maybe I was lying on it funny. No, Matt was pressing down too hard.

"Get off me." I sounded fretful.

"I will, I promise. Just as soon as I stop this bleeding."

What bleeding? I yawned again. Matt was getting blurrier and blurrier and I couldn't see much of him anymore, just his face. Suddenly, I remembered what I needed to know.

"Katy?"

"You saved her. Just hang in, please, Maddy. Don't die. Please don't die."

Matt made a sound like he was crying, but he was a long way away and I couldn't really tell. I was scared. Was I going to die? I could hear an ambulance going off in dark. The darkness felt like the feathered rear of a hen.

* * *

"Maddy?"

It was a woman's voice, my mother's but it couldn't be. What would she be doing here in the middle of the night? She wasn't due back until tomorrow afternoon. But when I opened my eyes fully I could see that it was no longer night-time, it was morning. No, not morning. I was in a brightly lit hospital room with a blocked nose – no, a tube – and another running into my hand. My chest hurt, or rather my shoulder. I couldn't move it. Something heavy was lying on it. I tried to touch it, but I was stopped by a fat bandage. Mum and Katy were on one side of my bed. Winona was on the other.

"Are you awake?" Mum was all rumpled linen and sitting on one of those institutional tub chairs and she had my hand, the one without the snaking bubbling tube, and she was crying.

"Oh, honey," she rested her forehead on my hand, overcome. I looked over at Katy to say, hey, our intellectual, no-nonsense mother was a blubbering mess. But she was crying too, silently. Winona stood on the other side of my bed. She was a wraith in a white cotton nightgown, the one she had on the night before last when I heard her crying. She wasn't crying this time. She was implacable, as usual. I said to her, "I'm glad to see you," wanting to give her the Taylor shake but unable to move my hand. She didn't answer, either. She didn't seem to hear.

"Oh, baby. Honey, thank god," Mum said, caressing my arm. She pulled herself together, blew her nose noisily into the edge of a tissue. "I thought you were going to die. I don't think I could bear it if I lost you, too."

Then another voice at the back of the room, firm and authoritative, the voice of a nurse in charge.

"She probably can't hear you."

"Yes, she can," Katy interrupted. "Look, she's trying to speak. You can see her lips move."

"Don't try to talk, Madison," said the nurse, and I could tell from her crisp tone she wanted the family out of the room so she could administer whatever it was that would send me back to sleep.

She swooped in to adjust the bag hanging from my metal bedhead.

"Her body has been through a tremendous trauma."

That had the opposite effect that the nurse had intended. Instead of tiptoeing obediently out of the room, my implacable mother began to cry more, stroking my arm so hard it hurt. I turned away. All this emotion was beginning to exhaust me.

I stared at Winona on the other side of the bed. She still wasn't crying. I wanted to say something to her, something important, but I couldn't make up my mind what that was. I fixed her with my eye and mouthed the word.

"What was that? What did she say?" Mum had also seen my lips move. Katy leaned in. Her eyes were red from crying. She watched my mouth carefully.

"Sorry. She said, sorry."

I kept my eyes fixed on Winona to gauge if she'd heard. Had she understood? I blinked. When I next looked, Winona was gone.

"Oh, honey." Mum's eyes welled up again. "Listen to me." She stroked my hand, the good one. "None of this was your fault. You looked after everyone beautifully like I knew you would."

The nurse swooped in again. "I think that's enough." She checked the monitor. "Look, her blood pressure is up, we don't want that."

I attempted to grasp my mother's hand. "Don't leave me, too."

She kissed my forehead and reluctantly stood up. "Katy and I will be just outside, we won't go anywhere. Get some sleep. We love you, honey."

I laid back against the pillows in the flickering light of the hospital room. I could hear the air conditioning rattling around behind the walls, but I was hot. I thrashed under my sheet and cell blanket. I tried to take it off, but my shoulder hurt too much. I heard the woman in the room next to me, coughing. She couldn't sleep, either. I turned my head and in the half-dark that would never leave me I saw the familiar red book.

It would be four thousand pages long, it said, if it talked about every woman who had been killed by a boyfriend.

It was morning next time I woke and I was just as tired as the night before, but achy and sore all over. I let my eyes wander over my room, half expecting to see Mum. I saw a bag hooked up to a metal hat stand next to a jug of water. Then I remembered what had happened last night, saw the fine spray of red across the beige door and a flash of orange nail polish. I closed my eyes and wished I'd died too.

* * *

"Only family members are allowed in." The next time I opened my eyes a young nurse, a trainee, was bending over me to adjust the drip. "But there's a tall handsome man outside your door. He's been there all night and I think he'd like to see you. Just for a minute." The nurse strapped a blood pressure cuff to my upper arm and it began to inflate. When she was satisfied that a non-regulation guest wouldn't interfere too much with my vital signs, she left the room.

Matt looked lousy. His eyes were bleary, his shirt was hanging out and there was stubble on his cheeks. He hovered in the doorway like he was afraid to come any closer. I gave him a grimace, the best I could do for a smile. He approached the bed cautiously and stood in front of the chair my mum had sat in.

"Maddy." His voice got trapped in his throat. He cleared it, started again, "I'm sorry." He ran his hand across his face, let it drop to his side, breathed out. I lifted my fingers. He lightly touched the back of my hand, the one without all the tubes. I choked. When I could speak, I said, "Winona's dead," and swallowed snot.

"I know." He bent his head.

"But I keep seeing her."

Matt nodded like he understood. He took my hand, lifted it up and softly kissed the back of it then gently laid it down again on the bed.

"How's Jess? Is she …?"

"She's in shock, but fine, thank god. Mum's with her."

"And Paris?"

Matt nodded his head again. "She's in a bad way, but they think she'll live."

Thank god.

The nurse bustled in. "Time's up. Madison needs to rest."

Matt began to back away towards the door. He had his hand on the lever.

"Wait," I said. I wiped my face with the back of my good hand, the one he'd just kissed.

"Thanks for saving me. I didn't get to say it before, you know, afterwards, when I was lying outside and you were, like, applying CPR and all that and everything. The doctor said that I would have bled to death if you hadn't kept it together and applied pressure with your T-shirt."

He saluted and shut the door behind him.

Afterwards, I dozed, waking again at dusk, disorientated and sore.

"You're looking a little better," said the sister as she readjusted my bandages. She'd just come on duty, taking over from the young nurse with the watery blue eyes and the allergies. This one was older and wore navy polyester culottes that whooshed whenever she moved.

"Where's my mum?"

"She'll be back soon." The sister replaced the pen in the ring at her name tag.

"Are you ready for something to eat?"

"I'm not really hungry."

"Okay, let me know when you are." She left the room. The door opened 30 seconds later and I didn't look up, expecting it to be the nurse again.

"Maddy."

"Dad!"

Dad hugged me like he never wanted to let me go.

"Dad, you're hurting me," I squirmed.

"Sorry." He released me with a kiss on my forehead. "I'm very glad to see you."

I just stared at him. His normally handsome face was grey and sunken. He hadn't shaved. He looked about 10 years older. But neither of us mentioned the reason why.

"Is Gary here?"

"He's parking the car. We got in the car and drove down as soon as we heard about what happened …" He choked, unable to finish. Gary came into the room, then, put his hand on Dad's shoulder briefly and leaned in to kiss me, too.

"Hi, kiddo," he said. "I hear you saved your sister's life." His eyes were full of pity and love.

I just shook my head. "No, I didn't."

* * *

Later that evening, I had another visitor. My dinner tray had just been removed and Dad and Gary had taken Katy back to the motel. Mum was with the hospital administrator organising for a rollaway bed to be put in my room for the night and to find out when she could take me – and Winona's body – back to Sydney.

"Madison?" A nurse appeared. She held my hand like she was about to take my pulse.

"A boy is here to see you. He says his name is Liam. Shall I wait until your father or mother come back before I send him in?"

I shook my head, "It's okay, send him in." I wanted to see him.

"Hi, Maddy." Liam looked emotional standing in the doorway. "Um, thanks for seeing me."

"Sure." I stared at Sinclair's best friend, who, while Sinclair sat in a police station, was here. He was nice looking with dark eyes and dark brown hair that curled around his ears. He was holding a bunch of flowers. I didn't ask him to sit down or try to take the flowers.

"How are you feeling?" He sat uncomfortably in the chair, still holding the flowers.

"Like I probably look." I saw him wince.

"I wanted to say …" He got up. "This was a mistake. I'm sorry," and put down the flowers on the table over my knees. But still he didn't go. He just stood there. Eventually, he spoke, his voice low. "I love her." He paused, shook his head, "I mean, loved her, you know, like really, really, in love with her. She loved me too." He looked at me then.

"I know."

He sort of smiled at that and drew a ragged breath. "How can I possibly live without her," and my heart went cold for I'd heard that someplace else, a lifetime ago, in a battered caravan, from the lips of someone who also said he loved my sister. Liam didn't appear to notice that I'd gone kind of still. He swiped at his eyes and said, "Sorry, I promised your mum I wouldn't upset you." He glanced at my bandaged shoulder. "Does it hurt much?" I gave him that look: what do you think? He nodded a bit, stepped towards the door.

"But you're going to be all right?"

"Doctors said I was lucky, the pellets lodged in the ball of my shoulder but missed all my major organs and arteries," I said dully.

"How long do you have to stay here?" But I couldn't tell him that or when Winona's funeral would be. I couldn't tell him much.

"Sinclair?" His name a question on my dry lips.

"Police have him. They found him in the games room, gibbering about his ears ringing and how the gun jammed, gunpowder still on his clothes." Liam sounding sad, rather than bitter.

Just as he reached the door, he turned and said, "I knew it was going to hit Sinclair hard. Winona and I. But I thought he'd take it out on me. I didn't know that anything like this would happen." He shook his head. "When Sinclair didn't show up at training I thought at first he was avoiding me. Then a few other things came out." He ran a hand through his hair. "And I started to get a bad feeling, thought that maybe – so I texted Winona to warn her he might head down to Paradise." His voice cracked. "If only I'd come down then, maybe I could have saved her." He rubbed his face with the heel of his hand, looked across at me, shook his head once as if clearing it. "You really do look like her," and he left the room.

Chapter 24

Six months later, I still couldn't move my arm above my ear. But I was alive. My sister, who wasn't, visited me regularly. She never spoke, just stood there in the half-light in the corner of my room or bathroom mirror, a silent wraith in bare feet and a white gown. I didn't mention this to anyone. According to the grief counsellor, the key to dealing with grief lay in the acceptance of death. I didn't imagine seeing her ghost signified acceptance. But it might be explained by the guilt which, sometimes, felt even worse than the grief and anger.

Sinclair, who was very much alive, also haunted me. His empty eyes and the way he smiled just before he pulled the trigger. What did he say to the police, the nervous rookie first on the scene?

"I just killed a girl. She deserved all she got, still didn't stop the pain. But I didn't have the guts to put the gun to my own head. That's fucked up."

He didn't mention Mal, whose body would wash up on Sapphire beach three days later. Or hurting Paris and me. But, why would he? He had been obsessed with only Winona. The rest of us were just *collateral damage*.

The letter about his sentencing hearing arrived one Thursday afternoon, the same day that Matt was due to visit. There it was, lying on the kitchen table, the corner wedged beneath the salt shaker and a cold cup of coffee like my mum couldn't bear to even touch it as she read it, when I came home from school.

I was supposed to go with friends to Westfield shopping straight after but I couldn't face the thought of escalators so I came home instead.

I threw down my bag, into the corner, and got a tub of yoghurt from the fridge. I never used to like yoghurt, but for some reason now I couldn't get enough of it. While I ate it – creamy mango and vanilla – I contemplated the letter. I didn't read it, though. I didn't need to. The crown prosecutor had already prepared us for what would be in it.

Several charges had been laid; the main one being that of murdering my sister, though they don't call it that in legal circles. The correct terminology is "assault occasioning actual bodily harm". This was utter bullcrap. Why soften the blow? Bodily harm suggested something not fatal. A bitch slap, perhaps, or a kick in the balls. Something survivable at any rate. I mean, murder's murder. You can't come back from being dead, right?

There were also several other charges, pointless ones, to my mind, but there all the same: possessing an unregistered firearm (Mal, or Mal's father, hadn't bothered to register his own shotgun); possessing ammo without a licence; using an unregistered firearm; and – my personal favourite – not keeping a firearm safely, an understatement if ever I heard one. There was also a charge of theft. Apparently, police found Winona's bracelet in the back pocket of his jeans.

Sinclair would be pleading diminished responsibility. They spoke of a psychotic episode, addiction to pills, Winona's promiscuity, access to violent video games, a stint in the army reserves, stress, you name it. I pictured him in court, smiling that $10,000 smile, while my beautiful sister turned to dust in the Northern Suburbs Cemetery, and I was nearly sick. If it wasn't his fault, then whose was it?

I took a spoonful of yoghurt and heard the floorboards in the study creak – since Winona's death Mum had been working from home. She soon appeared in the kitchen to begin burning the pork chops and undercooking the peas for dinner.

Afterwards, I knew, we'd eat cookie dough ice cream straight from the container.

We both ignored the letter, lying between us.

"You're home early from shopping," she said, screwing a silver earring into her right ear.

"I didn't end up going," I said as nonchalantly as possible. It didn't fool Mum for a second.

"Still can't face those escalators, huh?"

"Hmmm." I neither agreed nor disagreed, but Mum knew exactly how I felt. Some days were better than others. Some days, we'd go almost nuts with the pain. Either that or die. Then we'd wake up to another day and, somehow, the pain wouldn't be so bad. Katy, at least, had stopped crying herself to sleep.

The funeral had been the worst, far worse than going on an escalator. But I'd expected that. Winona's coffin. The house filled with flowers and casseroles. Mourners. Mum, grief making her shake like she had Parkinson's disease. Dad and Gary, both grey and stooping. The media *circus*. A 17-year-old girl with her whole life to live for killed in the blink of an eye by an entitled boyfriend with a loaded gun. It was news, all right. An online avalanche that distressed Katy so much that Mum made her give up all social media.

At least I got to see Matt, who'd come up for the funeral. He brought Jess, dressed demurely in black, her hair tied back and no rings in her nose.

"Thanks for coming," I had said to both of them afterwards, at the house, but looking only at Matt. It was Jess who answered.

"Yeah, yeah, absolutely," she said, and when I just looked at her, she added, "Here let me take that for you," and relinquished the plastic plate of cucumber sandwiches that teetered from one hand, my other incapacitated on account of my arm being in a sling. "Why don't I hand them out, leave you two alone." But not in a bitchy way, more conciliatory, as in I'm really, really sorry.

"Wow," I said staring after her. "That's different."

"Yeah. Maddy?" Matt started to say.

I turned back to him.

"There you are." A high pitched thin voice I recognised as my aunt's. "Can I borrow you? Your mother needs you," and I had been whisked away. And that had been that. And, except for Skype, the only contact I'd had with Matt.

Until tonight.

He'd applied to the Conservatorium of Music next year and had been given an audition and interview. It was tomorrow, and tonight he was staying here. And if he got in, he'd be moving here permanently. A full-time Sydneysider. My heart began a game of hopscotch inside and I closed my eyes waiting for it to pass.

"Maddy?" I opened my eyes and saw Mum looking at me curiously.

"I said, 'How are you feeling about Matt's visit?'"

I took a breath. What could I say? Truthfully, I didn't know how I felt about it. Good, mostly, but then I wasn't. I was confused. That was another symptom of grief, apparently. Normal everyday life felt uncertain all the time. All I knew for sure was that I felt comfortable with him. Since the funeral we'd Skyped a lot. He was still the same funny and great guy. He was patient, too. He understood my guilt at being alive when Winona was dead; guilt that while Sinclair was lining her up in his sights, we were kissing on a picnic table. He knew that I had been blown into tiny little pieces that couldn't be put back together in the same way they had once been. I knew I loved him. But did I still *love* love him? I wasn't sure.

Mum gave me an encouraging smile.

"It's okay to be confused."

She leaned in to hug me. "It's also okay for your life to go on."

As I breathed in Bulgari Green Tea mingled with garlic from dinner, I mumbled, "I just don't want you to resent me."

She pulled back to examine me. "Why on earth would I resent you?"

"I don't know. For being here. Being alive." I couldn't quite meet her eyes.

"Oh, darling." Then she put two hands on my cheeks to make me look at her. "Never, never think that.

Sinclair did a terrible thing. And he would have done it if I was there or not." She paused.

"Do you want to know what gets me up every morning?" and when I shook my head, "You and Katy. And, honey? I want you to live, be happy. And," she added, brushing hair from my eyes, "it's normal and completely natural to want that for yourself, too."

She gave another small compassionate smile, then a little push. "Why don't you get ready?"

As I reached the door, she said, "I almost forgot. Gary called before."

Another positive thing that had emerged from the ashes: Dad and Gary had begun coming around on a Friday night with dinner which we'd all eat together at the kitchen table with Mum in a kind of post-apocalyptic version of a family, and our salvation. I hoped his call didn't mean he was cancelling tomorrow night's meal.

"He wants to know if he should make chili con carne for tomorrow night." Mum began to take off her earring. "Will I tell him, yes?"

"Fantastic," I said.

In my room, I stripped off to my bra and underpants and stepped closer to the mirror above the chest of drawers. I still looked the same. Same long blunt fringe and olive eyes. I hadn't grown any taller either. But my face was more defined, more grown up. I slid down my bra strap so I could see the puckered scar. I put my finger on it.

My phone began to jump around on the dresser. I picked it up. It was a text from Matt.

In taxi. 2CH is on radio. Help me.

I thought for a minute, lower lip in my teeth. Typed back:

Can't help. Try 000.

A few seconds later: *They won't help either. Bad music is not an emergency, apparently.*

I typed back: *No tip for the driver then.*

His response: *2 late. Already tipped him and outside yr front door.*

Holy crap. I threw my phone on the bed, pulled on my second best jeans – the first were in the wash – and a blue stripy T-shirt, swiped mascara through my lashes, a brush through my hair. I breathed into my cupped hands to smell my breath, judged it okay, then to make sure sprayed Winona's bottle of *Daisy* and walked through the mist. I skidded down the tiled hallway in socks and flung open the door.

There he was, standing on the front step. He was wearing a rumpled suit jacket that looked like he'd plucked it from a St Vincent de Paul rack, over a black T-shirt and skinny jeans. A black suitcase on wheels sat by his boots and he was holding a wilting bunch of baby's breath with a couple of yellow rosebuds poking out. His hair was longer than it had been at the funeral, messily tied back and he'd tucked a couple of loose strands behind his ears. He had an earring. That was new. Other than that he looked just the same.

"These are for you," and he held out the flowers.

"They're beautiful." I took them and put my nose down to smell them. They smelled of plastic.

"No they're not. But they were the best I could do in the domestic terminal at 7pm."

"Well, thank you anyway." I leaned in to kiss him on the cheek. But he moved his face so that our lips touched lightly. He let me go, picked up his case but got no further because Katy had come out of her room.

"I've just been speaking to Paris. She says 'hi'," spied Matt on the doorstep, "Matt!" and wrapped her arms around his waist. "Guess what? You're sleeping in my room. I'm going in with Maddy."

"Hey, Katy." He hugged her back. "Man, you're all grown up. You look 14 at least"

She rolled her eyes, "Matt, I *am* 14."

"Thank god for that, then." Matt gave her his slow, sardonic grin. My stomach did flip flops. I looked at him and saw him for who he really was; a good guy. Not a hero, just a guy.

That was the other thing I learned at Cub Scouts. Survival.

I had done my own rescuing. I hadn't been able to save Winona and I would have to live with that for the rest of my life. But I had saved myself, and I'd saved Katy. And that felt good.

As Matt squeezed my fingers that were entwined with his, I realised I felt pretty good about him, too.